MYSTERIES IN OUR NATIONAL PARKS

THE HUNTED

GLORIA SKURZYNSKI AND ALANE FERGUSON

NATIONAL GEOGRAPHIC SOCIETY

WASHINGTON, D.C.

To Carrie Hunt—
who taught us to believe in the magic of her dreams—
and to her canine partners
Rio, Tuffy, Oso, Eilu, Blaze, Carmen, Yoki, Jewel,
Fancy, Usko, and especially Cassie.
Each day they demonstrate courage,
faithfulness, and above all, love.

Text copyright © 2000
Gloria Skurzynski and Alane Ferguson
First paperback edition 2001

Maps by Carl Mehler, Director of Maps;
Thomas L. Gray, Martin S. Walz, Map Research and Production
Bear paw art by Stuart Armstrong

This is a work of fiction. Any resemblance to living persons or events other than
descriptions of natural phenomena is purely coincidental.

Library of Congress Cataloging-in-Publication Data
Skurzynski, Gloria
    The hunted / Gloria Skurzynski and Alane Ferguson.
    p. cm. — (National parks mystery : #5)
    Summary: The Landon family travels to Glacier National Park to investigate
why grizzly bear cubs are disappearing and becomes involved with a ten-year-old
Mexican runaway boy.
        ISBN 0-7922-7053-3 (hardcover)
        ISBN 0-7922-7665-5 (softcover)
1. Glacier National Park (Mont.)—Juvenile fiction. [1. Glacier National Park (Mont.)—
Fiction. 2. National parks and reserves—Fiction. 3. Grizzly bear—Fiction.
4. Bears—Fiction. 5. Runaways—Fiction. 6. Mystery and detective stories.]
    I. Ferguson, Alane. II. Title. III. Series.
PZ7.S6282Hu 2000   99-048124
[Fic]—dc21

Printed in the United States of America

ACKNOWLEDGMENTS

The authors are most grateful to the following

staff personnel at Glacier National Park who

so generously shared their expertise: USGS

researcher Kate Kendall; wildlife biologist Steve

Gniadek; ranger Alison Disque; chief interpretive

ranger Larry Frederick; ranger Reggie Altop;

and Carrie Hunt of the Wind River Bear Institute.

Carrie's Web site is: http://www.beardogs.com

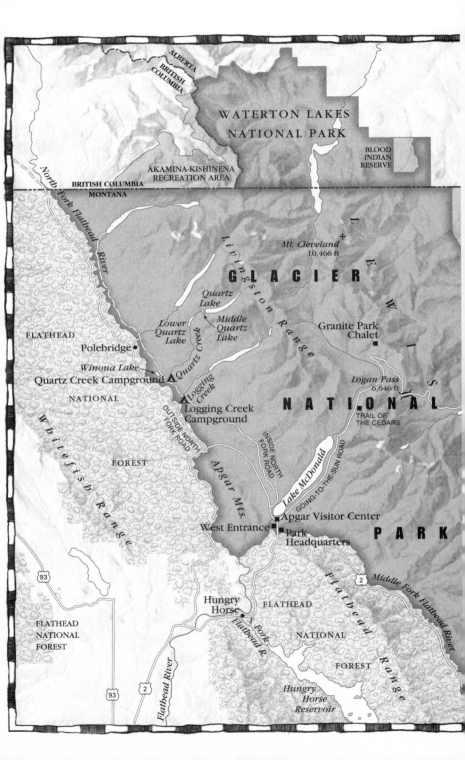

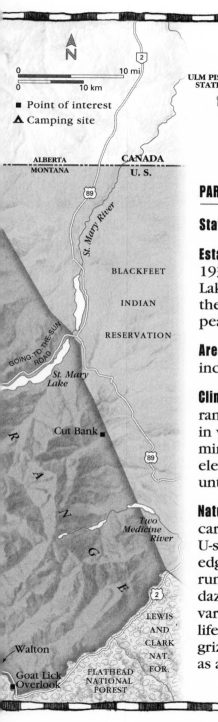

- ■ Point of interest
- ▲ Camping site

PARK DATA

State: Montana

Established: 1910; joined in 1932 with Canada's Waterton Lakes National Park to create the world's first international peace park

Area: 1,013,572 acres (does not include area in Canada)

Climate: In summer, temperatures range from 30°F to 90°F; in winter, temperatures reach minus 40°F; trails at higher elevations may be snowed-in until mid-July

Natural Features: Ice Age glaciers carved the park's lakes, U-shaped valleys, and knife-edged rock walls. In summer, runoff from glaciers creates dazzling waterfalls. The rich variety of plant and animal life — including some 200 grizzlies — led to its designation as a world heritage site.

Heavy metal blared through the cab of the van, so loud it rattled the coffee cup sitting on the dashboard.

"Hey, Max, shut off that radio," the driver shouted.

"Why?"

"Just do it. We ought to be getting sounds from back there about now, but I can't hear anything over all that music."

"Yeah, well...." Max looked uncomfortable. "Maybe they shoulda been awake even before this. See, Terry, I...uh...kinda took it easy on the drug."

"You what?" With a squeal of tires, the van screeched to a halt along the edge of the highway.

"I didn't want to overdose them. You know, 'cause they're pretty young," Max apologized.

"You idiot!" Terry raged, tearing off his dark glasses to shoot murderous glances at Max. "Go back there and check how they're doing."

Quickly, Max kicked open the passenger door and ran to the back of the delivery van. Unlocking the double doors, he swung them wide. Then he yelled. "Holy—! You won't believe this, Terry. You better get back here."

CHAPTER ONE

Was it happening? Was that what he felt—the first stirring of the earth beneath his hands and feet? Crouched under the hide of a dead buffalo calf, he commanded his tense body to remain still. No movement. Not until the right moment.

Now he was sure he felt it. He began to hear it, too. First a murmur, a muted pounding of thousands of hoofs. Then, like the swelling of ceremonial drums, a growing rumble. Did he dare turn his head to see how close the buffalo were? Better not: One movement too soon might send his own scent, the smell of 12-year-old boy, toward the big bull leading the stampeding herd to the cliff.

Now? The roar of hoofs, the lowing and snorting of the huge animals, the cries of frightened calves—all of it stabbed his hearing and took away his breath.

Now! First scrambling on all fours, then sprinting in

a crouch, he bellowed like a lost calf, praying that the lead cow would think he was a calf and turn toward him. Straight for the edge of the cliff he ran, terrified but at the same time exhilarated.

To the shortsighted buffalo dashing at full speed behind him, the ground ahead would appear to rise gently, like a low hill. By the time the buffalo herd finally saw the cliff, saw that the surface dropped off into nothingness, it would be too late. The lead bull and the lead cow would plunge over the edge, with most of the herd following, each animal plummeting through emptiness until they all lay smashed on the rocks beneath.

Just ahead of the panic-stricken animals, the boy himself would leap over the cliff. But he would be safe. If he had great skill, and if the Buffalo Spirit guided him, he would land on a ledge beneath the rim of the cliff.

How many times had be practiced his dash to the precipice? He knew where the ledge was, the jutting tongue of rock that would save him. Yet what if he stumbled, or rolled away from the right spot? He would die, too, broken on the bloody ground far below, next to the dead buffalo.

They were only inches behind him now. The ground's violent shaking nearly knocked him off his feet. It was the moment—he leaped! Flew over the edge! Landed hard. Clawed with fingers and moccasins to secure his hold on the jagged jut of rock. The hide of the dead calf flew away from him, revealing his own tangle of black hair....

"Hey, who left the door of the camper open?"

"What?" His daydream shattered, Jack Landon pulled himself back to the present. His fantasy—of being a buffalo runner—faded quickly, like a switched-off TV program.

"Jack, are you listening to me? Close the trailer door and make sure it latches. We don't want it flying open while we're driving."

"OK, Dad."

The Landons had just spent an hour at the visitor center of Ulm Pishkun State Park, in Montana, to learn about the Great Buffalo Jump. A thousand years earlier, buffalo had been stampeded by Native American hunters. Then, after a chase of a mile or more, they were lured to their death by a brave buffalo runner who led them over the same cliff the Landons could see clearly from the visitor center.

Jack had listened to stories about boys no older than he was, boys who disguised themselves under buffalo hides and brought the herd to its destruction. Would he have been brave enough to try that? To plunge off a cliff and risk his life clinging to a ledge while those big buffalo hurtled over his head?

"Hop in the Jeep," his father called again. "We have a long drive ahead if we're going to make it to Glacier National Park before dark."

Jack and his sister climbed into the backseat, each closing the door gently on the side where they sat. It had turned into a contest to see who could close a door more quietly and still make it latch. The game had started earlier on this trip after their parents told them to stop slamming the doors.

Jumping into the front seat, Olivia said, "I'm glad we stopped to find out about the buffalo jump. Now— let's take off for grizzly bear country."

"Yahoo!" Jack cried, excited at the prospect of actually seeing a grizzly. He knew the powerful animals were shy, and that he probably wouldn't see any more than a picture of them in the Glacier visitor center. Still, he could hope. "Mom," he asked, "how many grizzlies do they have at Glacier?"

"Probably about 200. With this new DNA program in the park, they should get an accurate count pretty soon. Look," Olivia said, turning in her seat and holding up a newspaper. "There's an article on page 3 about the bear-identification project. I'm going to meet with the woman heading the research—Kate Kendall. I think she's quoted in here."

Jack took the paper, slumped back into his seat, and began to read the Missoula [Montana] *Missoulian*. Dated June 24, it had been published just the day before. As he opened it to the third page, he tried to fold the pages neatly, but newspapers are like road maps—they always fight back. Soon he grew absorbed in the article.

It was about a U.S. Geological Survey team setting traps throughout the park—not dangerous traps, just barbed wire strung about two feet high. A bear, drawn by a scent lure, would step over the wire to reach the scent. When the bear pulled back, hair from under its neck would catch on the barbs. Project scientists collect the bear hair and take DNA readings of it, using complicated lab techniques to get each bear's DNA "fingerprint."

"Will this be part of what you're doing at Glacier?" Jack asked his mother. Olivia Landon was a wildlife veterinarian who traveled to U.S. national parks when there was a problem with animals.

"I think so," she answered. "But mostly I'm supposed to figure out why there's such a shortage of grizzly cubs—one-and-a-half-year-olds, the ones in their second summer. Their numbers are way down, and nobody can figure out why. The whole thing is a real mystery." The skin between her eyebrows furrowed as she added, "I just hope I can help find the answer."

"You will," Steven assured her, reaching over to rub the back of her neck. "With you, Glacier National Park will get the best help there is."

Ashley tugged Jack's arm impatiently. "Hey, are you done with the paper?"

"In a second. I'll give you the page that tells about the bear DNA project, though."

Her face clouding, Ashley shook her head, then

looked out the window at the open plains rolling by. The colors were a mix of soft yellows and dusty greens, which stretched endlessly across hills that looked as soft as pillows. Blue sky reached down and touched the tops of the hills, but Jack knew his sister wasn't interested in all of this quiet beauty. For some reason she didn't want to look at the article he was trying to hand her.

"What? You don't want to learn about bears?" Jack prodded.

"No. It's just—there's more going on than stuff with grizzlies. All you guys can talk about are bears, bears, bears. I want to think about something else for once."

"Yeah, like what?"

"If you let me have the paper—"

"What's wrong, Ashley? Are you scared? Are you afraid a big grizzly's going to come into the tent and eat you?"

"Stop it, Jack. Don't be dumb." Ashley scowled at him, moving as far to her side of the Jeep as she could. For once they had plenty of room. Most often when the Landons drove to the different national parks, they had one or more foster children with them; Olivia and Steven were certified emergency-care foster parents. But on this trip the Landons were alone, and Jack liked it that way.

"OK, Ashley wants us to talk about stuff besides bears. Let's see, what else is in the paper? Hmmm. What can I find…?" Jack knew Ashley was getting mad, but he couldn't help teasing. It was in his job description as a big brother. Besides, Ashley had been acting kind of edgy toward him.

"This article says the government is going to dust for tree beetles. Wow, that's interesting."

"Knock it off," his sister told him.

"I'm trying to be helpful." He gave her one of his biggest smiles, but she just rolled her eyes.

"Mom, will you tell Jack to give me the paper?"

"Hey, here's something really interesting on the back page," he commented, still holding the newspaper out of Ashley's reach. "A Mexican kid, ten years old—that's the same as you, Ashley—sneaked across the border into the United States three times. Twice he got caught and was sent back to Mexico, but he's made it across again, and they think he might have come all the way up here to Montana. Uh-oh."

"What?" Ashley asked, eyeing him suspiciously.

"He made it all the way up here, and then…a bear ate him."

"He was eaten? Are you serious?" Olivia asked, turning in her seat.

"Just kidding, Mom. At least about the bear part. I like to bug Ashley."

"Well, you're doing a good job of it," Steven said.

"Can't you two share the newspaper?" their mother asked.

"Never mind, she can have it." Jack tossed the paper at Ashley. "When are we going to stop for lunch, Dad?" he asked. "I'm starving."

"Jack, we just got started on this leg of the trip," Steven answered impatiently. "I don't want to stop for a couple more hours."

"You're hungry because you didn't finish your breakfast," Olivia told him. "You wasted half your scrambled eggs."

"I wasn't in the mood for them."

Sighing, Olivia said, "Fine. There's trail mix and bottled water in the tailgate."

As Jack unzipped a baggie and poured a handful of trail mix, he started to think again about the buffalo, how the tribes used every part of it—the meat for food, the hides for clothes and teepees and moccasins, the horns for bows. Nothing went to waste. Everything had a use, even the tail was used for chasing flies. The buffalo had become the very heartbeat of the tribes.

Jack thought about the buffalo runner, the brave boy who risked his life to help his people. Would he, Jack, have the same kind of raw courage? As the tires purred softly on the smooth highway, he put his head back and drifted once again into his daydream.

CHAPTER TWO

Never in his life had Jack seen quite the shade of shimmering blue that filled Lake McDonald. As he stood with his family on the shore, his eyes swept across crystal clear water the color of turquoise, reflecting sky and clouds. The lake stretched in a nine-mile oval ringed by a forest of thick pine that erupted into gigantic glaciated mountains. Everything around it was heavy with color, from the jewel-like wildflowers that bloomed against the shore to the lavender, blue, and yellow stones that pebbled the ground. The sweet smell of pine filled his every breath. It was perfect.

"Those woods are thick," Ashley murmured.

"I know," Olivia agreed. "It's nothing short of paradise. Have you ever seen water so clear? It's as if you were looking through glass."

"Can we swim in it?" Jack asked. After the long drive from Ulm Pishkun, his skin itched with perspiration, and his feet felt hot in their shoes. Ashley, he knew, was just as warm. The Jeep's air conditioner barely pushed out enough stale air to keep his parents cool in the front seat.

As they'd made their long descent through the mountains into Glacier National Park, Ashley's nose had pressed flat against the window to search the tightly knit pines for any signs of bears. Out loud she'd wondered how bears could stand the heat with such thick coats of fur, when she could hardly take it in a pair of shorts and a T-shirt.

Looking around now, Jack saw that although people clustered along the edge of Lake McDonald, not one of them was actually in the water. Fishermen cast off from land or farther out from canoes, their fishing lines catching the sun like long strands of spider web.

"I don't think you'd like to dive in there," Steven told Jack, shaking his head. "This is glacial water. You'd have about three minutes before you turned as blue as the lake. Go ahead, put your hand in and check it out."

Crouching low, Jack thrust his arm deep into water that felt as frigid as an ice chest. He pulled it out again quickly, shaking pearls of moisture off as he grinned and said, "So this is where frozen fish come from."

"Very funny," Steven chuckled. "Just make sure your sister doesn't fall in before we get back. We won't be long."

"Daddy, I *won't* fall in the lake. I'm not some little

kid. Besides, where are you going?" Ashley asked. "If it's to the gift shop, then I want to come, too. I want to get some bear bells."

Olivia answered, "Honey, you don't need any bear bells."

"But—"

"We're just going to the visitor center, right over there." Olivia jerked her thumb at a low-slung log building a few hundred yards behind them. "I'm too grubby to go into park headquarters right now. I'll be fresher in the morning." Their mother was dressed in denim shorts and a shirt that had wilted during the long drive. Strands of curly, dark hair escaped from her ponytail, which she shoved under her baseball cap while she spoke. Olivia was so small and trim, Jack thought she could pass for a college student. His father, all bones and angles, towered over Olivia. Steven's blond hair and blue eyes made a striking contrast to Olivia's darker coloring. The two of them were so different and yet, Jack realized, the same somehow. Ever since he could remember, it seemed as though his parents worked in tandem. They were a comfortable couple.

"But Mom, listen to me." Ashley's voice was rising now. "If we're going to camp way out in the woods, then we should wear bear bells."

"Don't worry about the bells, Ashley. They're not loud enough for the bears to hear."

"What are bear bells?" Jack broke in.

"Jingle bells that you strap onto your wrists or ankles," his mother answered. "They're supposed to warn a bear that you're coming through, but it's better to use your own voice and just call out every once in a while. Remember what I told you, bears won't bother us if we don't bother them."

Olivia arched her back, stretching after the long hours of driving. "Anyway, we've got to grab a map before the center closes so we can nail down exactly where Quartz Creek is. Your father wants to photograph the unspoiled beauty of Glacier, which means," she said, throwing a glance at Steven, "we have a long, bumpy ride ahead of us, through backwoods country."

"Hey, at least I'm willing to ask for directions." Steven grinned at her, then added, "How many guys do that?"

"Hardly any, which means you're this close"—she squeezed her thumb and pointer finger together—"to being perfect."

"Wow, look at that—I almost made it," Steven laughed. "OK, kids, we'll meet you back here at a quarter to. Don't wander off. We're going to have to really push to set up camp before dark, and I don't want to have to go looking for either one of you."

"Gotcha, Dad."

After they left, Ashley muttered to herself, "The book says bear bells work." While she perched on a tree stump close to shore, looking gloomy, Jack chose a smooth, plum-colored stone and skimmed it against the lake's surface. The rock skipped five times, not bad for a first try.

A flatter, topaz yellow stone grazed the lake, and he let out a holler. "Hey, Ashley, did you see that? Nine skips—that's a record for me. Come on and try. I'm telling you, the rocks here are perfect."

"No thanks," Ashley answered. With her hand shading her eyes, she peered intently at the west side of the lake. Jack stopped skimming stones long enough to ask, "What are you looking at?"

"Nothing."

The way she said it, Jack could tell it was not *nothing*. She was chewing on something in her mind. During the last hour of their drive to Glacier, every mile they'd traveled seemed to subdue her more, as if the mountains themselves were pressing down on her. That was unlike Ashley, who usually jabbered away like a magpie.

"If it's nothing, then why don't you come skip a couple of rocks?" he asked her.

"Because I'm thinking."

"Thinking about what?"

Hesitating, she said, "If I tell you, do you promise not to say anything to Mom?" She looked at him, half scared, half defiant. When Jack nodded, she said, "I'm...I'm watching out for grizzly bears. You know how Mom wouldn't let me read that book *Night of the Grizzlies* because she said it was too intense? Well, I read it anyway."

"Ashley—"

"I'm old enough. And I'm glad I did, 'cause even though Mom knows a lot, she doesn't know everything. You should put on bear bells because a grizzly can charge out of the woods and kill you fast as lightning. Those bears'll eat you!"

Jack crossed his arms as he studied his sister. He remembered the argument. Ashley had brought the book home from the library, and Olivia had immediately told her not to read it, explaining that she didn't want it to spook Ashley right before their trip. It was rare for their mother to say no to any book. This one was banned, Olivia said, only until they got back home to Jackson Hole. "Here, Ashley, try reading this instead," she'd suggested. "It's a book of Native American legends from around the Glacier area. This won't give you nightmares."

Reluctantly, Ashley had taken the folklore book and scanned the first page. She didn't answer when their mother asked, "Isn't that better than reading about those gruesome bear attacks?"

"So you're all freaked, just like Mom said you would be, right?" Jack asked Ashley now.

She nodded miserably. "I can't stop thinking about it. There's a few of them in the mountains around Jackson

Hole, where we live, but there's lots more of them up here. *Hundreds* of *grizzlies*." Her eyes squinted as she looked into the distance. "They could be right in those trees, watching us this very minute."

Jack snorted. "Look, McDonald Inn is right next to us, and behind that is a bunch of cabins, and up the road are two stores and a restaurant plus the visitor center. Quit worrying. There are way too many people around here for a bear to show up."

"You don't know anything about it," Ashley snapped back.

"Well, I know that the attacks in that book happened a long time ago, before we were even born. There's nothing to worry about. Forget it."

His sister's eyes flashed. "Just 'cause I'm younger than you doesn't mean I don't know what I'm talking about." Ashley's lips tightened. Her chin rested on her bent knees, while her toes extended beyond her sandals and curled over the edge of the tree stump she was sitting on. Dark hair skimmed forward to almost hide her face, but even so, Jack could see how pale she looked.

He dropped the fistful of damp skipping stones he'd been holding; they clicked against other rocks on the ground like rain on a tin roof. Walking to where she sat, he said, "What's going on, Ashley?"

"Nobody ever listens to what I think. It's like I'm too little, or what I say's not important. Did you know a girl was in her sleeping bag close to Lake McDonald, and this grizzly went right into her camp and dragged her off and ate her? She was only 18 years old. And on the exact same night, a different girl got chewed up in *her* sleeping bag, except that was up in a place called Granite Park Chalet only ten miles away. She died, too."

"That's sad, but so?"

"So maybe we *should* buy bear bells. Maybe Mom should stay out of the woods where the grizzlies are. Dad, too. Maybe it's too dangerous."

"Mom knows what she's doing," Jack countered. "She's a wildlife veterinarian."

"People all taste the same to a grizzly."

Jack wanted to laugh at that, but he pushed down his smile. "Look, this is the first trip we've had in a long time without some foster kid tagging along, and I want it to be good. We're going to camp and fish and hang out with the animals. Can you drop the bear stuff?"

"It's not just the bears," Ashley told him, standing up. "It's that *nobody* listens to me."

CHAPTER THREE

The road flowed over the mountains like a silver creek—here dividing homesteads, there cutting through wild pine and underbrush that crowded right to the edge of the asphalt until the road emptied into ranchland again. To Jack, it was strange to see so many private homes and cultivated fields at a national park, but his dad had told him the homesteads had been bought long before Glacier had been created as a park, so the families who were already there got to stay. Jack wished people hadn't marred the natural beauty, but then again, he'd jump at the chance to live in one of those log cabins that glowed with warm, yellow light in the midst of grassy meadows. He guessed he couldn't get too mad at the people who wanted to stay put.

"How much longer?" Ashley groaned.

Peering at the map, Olivia answered, "It looks like we're still about 15 miles away, and they told me the final 6 miles are going to be pretty rough. I wish that Dramamine worked on you better—you've always had to be different, haven't you?"

"Rougher than this? Great!" Ashley moaned louder, clutching her stomach.

Jack knew what his sister meant. With the trailer hitched to their car, it seemed every bump gave them whiplash. Ashley always got queasy from rolling motion. If the road ahead was even worse, she was really in for it. He was about to ask his dad if there was another way to the campground when their car slowed at a small ranger station that was not much bigger than a shed. A thin, weathered woman in a ranger hat leaned out of an open window. "May I see your park pass?" she asked.

"This is Olivia Landon, and I'm her husband, Steven, and that's Ashley and Jack. We're here from Jackson Hole, Wyoming—"

"Oh, yes, we've been expecting Mrs.—I mean Doctor—Landon. Hi, kids, welcome to Glacier."

Ashley gave a faint wave as Jack said, "Hi."

The ranger's skin had tanned to a nut brown, which made her gray eyes look extra bright in her square face framed by blunt-cut gray hair. Her hands looked rough but strong, and the muscles of her forearms stood out in thick ropes. According to the tag on her uniform, her name was Jane Beck. "Weird thing about those missing baby grizz," Jane said, leaning from the booth.

"I've been watching for them but haven't seen a single second-summer cub in, oh, I don't know how long. I'm glad the officials brought you in to help figure it out, Dr. Landon."

"Call me Olivia. Have you tracked any mother that still has her cubs?" Olivia leaned forward so that she could look the ranger in the eye.

Jane pushed her ranger hat back on her head. "I saw one in the area a while back with two cubs, but then all of a sudden the mom showed up alone. Early spring, I saw another sow with one cub. The mom had an odd coloration, something like a rugby stripe, so for fun I named her Polo and her little baby Marco. Anyway, I've seen her a couple of times since, but Marco's been missing. Then there's a ginger-colored mom with two babies, but I haven't seen them in ages. Hold on, just one minute." Jane's head disappeared, then reappeared with a map and a key. "Figured I'd better get your stuff, since it's getting close to dark and you've got a camper to set up."

Pointing to the road beyond, she said, "Up ahead, where the road makes a *T,* take a right. You'll be going through a burn area, then it'll green up again. Quartz Creek campground'll be about ten miles south of here, on your left. The camp is officially closed until the first of July, which means the entrance is chained—you'll need to unlock it to get in. When you leave, just chain it up again."

"No problem," Steven told her, taking the key from her outstretched hand.

"One more thing. There's a ranger station farther south from where you'll be staying, maybe four or five miles past. Other than that, you'll be all alone."

"Great—exactly what we want," Steven nodded.

"Alone as in people, but not alone as in bears. Adult grizz are still in these parts, so be careful." Holding up her hand, she ticked off the points on her fingers: "Don't leave food anywhere they can get at it; Keep your garbage locked inside your car at all times; Always walk in pairs, even when you're going to use the outhouse; Make noise when you hike. I'm sure you know all of this, but I'll feel better if I tell you one more time. Now, is there anything else I can help you with?"

"I'd like to interview you to find out more about what you've observed with those mamma bears and their cubs," Olivia told her.

"Sure. I'll be here tomorrow if you need me." She touched the brim of her hat and said, "I hope you can solve this mystery, Dr. Landon. For us, the grizzlies are like family."

As their car bumped along the road, Jack watched the land change in the waning twilight, not gradually like a suburb changes into a city, but suddenly, like the sea to a shore. Gone were the cottonwood trees and the endless lodgepole pine; gone were the islands of wild grass that bent their stalks to the wind and the clusters of wildflowers that dotted the meadows as if they were buttons on a silk dress. In their stead were the remains of charred trees, lifeless, silent. It felt to Jack as though he were entering a cemetery. Blackened spikes reached into the air, some erect, some broken into crazy angles, others toppled one against the other like fallen tombstones. There was a hush in the car as they stared at the charred emptiness.

"What happened?" Ashley breathed.

"A lightning strike."

"Why didn't the park people put it out?"

"You know, they used to put out every fire they could," Olivia answered, "but the truth is, it's a lot better for the environment just to let it burn."

"I don't get it," Ashley protested. "Why is it OK to let trees get killed?"

Steven quickly glanced over his shoulder and told Ashley, "I know it seems bad, but letting the land take care of itself is the best way to preserve it in the end. It's better for the trees, the other plants, and especially the animals. Like the bears. I've learned a lot about them since your mom's been doing her research. Did you know that grizzly bears don't really like the woods? They need open spaces—meadows and rangeland.

Shrugging, Ashley said, "So, what does that have to do with letting a fire turn the forest all ugly?"

"Everything," Olivia answered, twisting around in her seat. "When the settlers came into Montana and took over the lowlands for farming and grazing, the grizzlies had to move. They fled to the mountains, and they've adapted to living here, but it's not their first choice. So the grizz tend to hang out in the open places in the forest. You've seen a lot of meadows up here, right?"

Jack nodded. Glacier's thick woods were like a sea of evergreen broken up by meadow islands. He'd seen small lakes that shone like mirrors in the sun, lots of open grassland, then thickets of woods dotted by meadows again.

"OK," Olivia went on, "follow me here. The fires clear out space, meadows spring up in that space, and the grasses bring the little animals and a place for the huckleberries, which, in turn, bring the bears. Do you see how it's all connected?"

"The circle of life," Jack chimed in.

"Exactly," Olivia nodded. "The circle of life, which we shouldn't mess with. When the parks used to put out fires, the forests got heavy with dead trees, and the meadows were getting all crowded out. It took a while for folks to figure it out, so now when there's a fire, it's allowed to burn. And pretty soon Mother Nature will put it all back together again."

"Hey—do you think the missing baby grizzlies might have been killed in the fire that was here?" Jack asked, thinking that nothing much could survive the devastation of a searing forest fire. "Maybe that's what happened to them."

"No, believe it or not, forest fires aren't anything like what you've seen in the movie *Bambi*, where all the animals are running for dear life. Most of the animals leave ahead of the flames, and a few burrow underground and aren't even scorched, unless it's a really hot burn. That's not why the baby grizz are disappearing."

A shadow crossed Olivia's face, and Jack noticed smudges underneath her eyes. She was worried about the missing cubs, he knew. She'd spent countless hours researching the information the park had given her. All the way to Glacier she'd reviewed the material, studying bear-sighting records and weather patterns and bear-mortality numbers and plant-growth statistics, especially about the abundance of huckleberries, because they are the bears' favorite food. Doggedly, she'd searched for a clue the park officials might have overlooked. So far, she'd found nothing.

Tiny lines gathered in Olivia's forehead as she crinkled her brow. "You know, I can't help thinking about little Marco, and what's become of him. Jane's right: The grizzly are a threatened species here in the lower 48, and we can't spare even one of them. I just wish I knew what I was looking for."

"You'll fix it," Jack assured her.

"I hope so. Somebody's got to, or the number of grizzlies in this park will be seriously impacted in a few generations, and that would be a terrible loss to everyone."

"Except to the people who get eaten," Ashley muttered, under her breath. "Nobody cares about what happens to them."

"What did you say, Ashley?" their mother asked.

Ashley slumped in her seat. "Nothing."

"She said, 'Nobody cares about the people who get eaten,'" Jack offered, miffed that his sister sounded as though she didn't worry about the baby bears.

"Jack!" Ashley cried, punching his thigh at the same time their mom called out, "Ashley!"

"Hey!" Jack told his sister, "Knock it off!"

"Well, you shouldn't have told Mom."

"Then you shouldn't have said it!"

"Ashley," their mother began, but Ashley said hotly, "People do get eaten by grizzlies, so maybe it's better if the grizzlies go live someplace else! Why doesn't anybody care about the poor visitor who turns into bear food?"

"Sweetheart, we can't push the grizzlies out of Glacier just because people want to hike here—the bears need someplace to live, too. You know, this isn't like you. You've always loved every kind of animal." After a pause, their mother asked gently, "What is it, Ashley?"

When Ashley didn't answer, Jack stared at the floor of their car. His sneaker had a smudge of mud on one side that he rubbed against the floor mat. It was obvious Ashley was really bothered by that stupid grizzly book, but he'd told his sister he'd keep quiet about it, and that was almost the same as a promise. The best he could hope was that she'd spit it out and get the whole thing over with.

Outside, the living forest had returned, gray-green in the half-light, branches melting into other branches to create an awning of pine. Their Jeep pitched along the road, the front end bucking up first, and then the back end, like a crazed bull in a rodeo; then left to right, swinging wildly like a boat in rough water, at times scratching against the wild roses that flowered along the road's edge in bright pink splashes against the green. Ashley sat, sullen, her arms crossed over her white T-shirt in a tight clamp. Two braids bounced against her shoulders as the Jeep bumped along; Jack noticed curly bits of hair had managed to escape from her part to create a fuzzy halo. Her mouth was pressed shut as if to keep any sound from escaping.

"Aren't you going to talk to me?" Olivia asked.

Come on, just tell her, Jack pleaded in his mind. *It's not that big a deal. You're only making it worse.*

"She's not saying a word, so now I *know* something's wrong," Steven teased. "Hey, Ashley, I saw that look. You just rolled your eyes right at the ceiling—I can see you in my rearview mirror. Help me out here—isn't Jack the one who's supposed to get temperamental? *He's* the almost-teenager. Technically, there're three years to go before you go moody on me."

"*I'm* not moody—" Jack protested.

Ashley snorted, "Yeah, right," at which Jack reminded them that it was Ashley they were talking about, not him, to which Ashley replied that he, Jack, was always bossing her around. At that, Jack blurted out, "That's because you don't listen and do what you're supposed to. You went right on and read *Night of the Grizzlies* and got all freaky. Now you're ruining the vacation for the rest of us 'cause you've turned into a bear psycho."

His mother's mouth made a small *O* as she thought a moment, then said, *"Night of the Grizzlies*—is that what this is about? No wonder you're so spooked." Olivia turned around in her seat so that she could look Ashley full in the face. She didn't appear to be the least bit annoyed that Ashley had read something she wasn't supposed to. Instead, an expression of concern filled Olivia's face as she centered her chin over the back of the headrest. "Ashley, listen to me. The grizzlies that attacked those poor girls were fed by people all the time. That was the problem. They'd totally lost their fear of humans. You've got to remember that the tragedy happened a long time ago. Bears are managed very differently now."

"How?" his sister asked softly. Her eyes, wide and dark, were fixed on her mother.

"Well, in just about every way. Trust me. The park would never let that kind of thing happen nowadays— a bear like the ones in that book would be taken out of Glacier so fast it'd make your head spin. Today's Glacier grizzlies are truly wild, which means they steer clear of humans, just the way nature intended. Like I said, leave them alone, and they'll leave you alone. "

Biting the edge of her lip, Ashley said, "OK."

"Good. And I hope you'll also understand that when I tell you not to do something, it's for a reason. You've wasted a lot of energy over this. It could have ruined your stay in this beautiful park."

"You're right," Ashley agreed, relieved she was being let off the hook. "Thanks, Mom."

Olivia sat forward again and buckled her seat belt. They pitched and swayed the next four miles in silence, Ashley ever more queasy, Jack deep into his own thoughts. Suddenly, his father announced, "There's the sign—Quartz Creek Campground. Hey, kids, try reading that out loud five times really fast."

"Quartz Creek Campground," Ashley began, "Quartz Cweek Cwampgwound, Courts Cweek Cramp—I can't say it! Jack, you try!"

Jack's tongue felt all turned around inside his mouth as he tackled the phrase, but he didn't mind such silliness. He was glad the storm between him and his sister had blown over, that they were laughing and back to normal, with nothing more to worry about than keeping the mosquitoes away. He was still smiling as he grabbed his soda can from the backseat, where Ashley lingered while Steven and Olivia got out to unlock the chain stretched across the entrance.

"Hey Ashley, why are you sitting in there? Aren't you getting out?" Jack asked, gulping down the last of his soda. Warm fizz bubbled against the back of his throat.

"Sure. Now that you and I have a second alone, I just wanted to say one thing."

"What?"

Ashley leaned over so that her braids skimmed the backseat. Her face was so close to Jack's that he could feel her breath on his cheek. "I'm going to act just as nice to you as I ever did, but—" she took a breath, "I will never, ever tell you anything again as long as I live."

With that, she gave him one last look, got out of the car, and shut the door so softly it hardly made a sound.

CHAPTER FOUR

Each of you kids grab a flashlight. Stand at the edges of the flat area. Hold the flashlights toward me so I can see where to back in."

Dusk faded quickly into darkness as Steven pulled forward and backward several times, trying to position the trailer. Finally he got it on a nice, level spot. Then, by flashlight, he disconnected the trailer hitch and drove the Jeep out of the way, parking it next to a tall stand of Douglas fir.

"Now the hard part," Steven announced. "Wish we'd gotten here sooner so we'd still have a little daylight. Oh well...."

Jack and his dad worked as swiftly as they could. After they lowered the bottom section of the camping-trailer door, they released the latches that held the top down for travel.

Meanwhile, Olivia had crawled inside the Jeep. She

pulled boxes from the tailgate and turned to hand them to Ashley, except, where was Ashley?

"Holy cow! What was that?" Jack exclaimed. Out of the corner of his eye he'd caught sight of a dark shape exploding past him into the trees and had heard the snap of branches as the shadow disappeared into the underbrush.

A beat too late, Ashley answered from the darkness, "It was nothing."

"What do you mean nothing! It looked like a big dog or—"

"I saw it too," she said. "I was almost right next to it. It was a...baby deer."

"Are you sure?" Jack didn't know exactly what he'd seen rushing past him, but it hadn't looked anything like a fawn. And Ashley was acting strange again. "How could a baby deer be right next to us when we're doing all this work on the trailer?" he asked her.

"Why don't you come check it out, and then you can tell Mom and Dad all about it," Ashley said, with a hard glance in his direction. "I'm telling you what I saw. I was right here."

"OK, OK. A baby deer. The weirdest baby deer I've ever seen, but whatever you say, Ashley."

"Jack, we need to crank up the top now," Steven called. "Make sure none of the canvas gets caught on the edges at your end."

Still muttering to himself, Jack rotated the handle

that raised the roof of the camping trailer. Fully opened, it stretched tall and spacious: metal roof, canvas sides, metal base. Its two pull-out queen-size beds (one at either end) plus a smaller bench with a mattress provided comfortable sleeping for all the Landons. Steven joked that compared with real, rough-out camping, staying in their trailer was like renting a suite at a five-star hotel.

Olivia had already gone inside to set up the sink and stove top. She stacked plates into the cabinets, then unrolled all their sleeping bags onto the beds. Steven and Olivia would share one of the queens, and Jack and Ashley would take turns sleeping on the other queen and the bench.

"Hello, anybody home?" It was a woman's voice, but all Jack could see was a flashlight beam dancing against the dirt path. "Thought I'd check in to find out if you need anything."

Olivia came to the door holding an oil lantern that gave enough light to reveal their visitor—a park ranger in her 20s, dressed in the Park Service uniform: a Smoky Bear hat, gray shirt with badge and name tag, and dark green pants. Even in that dim light, Jack couldn't help noticing how pretty the ranger was. Beneath the hat brim, brown hair barely skimmed her shoulders. Her eyes were friendly and her smile bright.

"You must be Olivia," she said. "I'm Ali. I'm at the Logging Creek Ranger Station just a few miles south of here. The plan says that I'm supposed to pick you up tomorrow morning to drive you to park headquarters. So…." She looked up at Olivia, who was standing in the doorway of the trailer. "Is there anything I can do right now to help you set up?"

"Thanks, but I think we've got things under control," Olivia answered and introduced Ali to Steven and Jack. A look of concern passed over her face as she said, "Steven, where's Ashley?"

"I don't know. I thought she was with you, setting up the inside stuff."

"And I thought she was helping you and Jack. Ashley!" Olivia cried, then again, louder, *"Ashley!"*

"I'm right here, Mom. Don't worry, I'm coming. I was down there by the creek, looking at the water." Ashley emerged from behind a stand of pines, acting sheepish that she'd been caught loafing when there was work to be done.

"Ali, this is my daughter, Ashley, who knows better than to go off alone in the woods. Ashley, meet Ali. I was about to say that we're going to build a campfire so we can toast a few marshmallows. Can you stay awhile, Ali?"

"Sure. I never turn down marshmallows." Ali joined the Landons as they scouted for firewood by flashlight, moving noisily through the underbrush, snapping branches and twigs beneath their feet, trying not to trip over roots. Jack was surprised that Ashley didn't stick close to any of them; actually, for a few moments, he didn't see her at all. Then she turned up and dumped a meager armload of firewood on the ground.

When they got a small, steady blaze going and Olivia brought out the toasting forks, Ashley speared the soft, white marshmallows, one after the other, onto the prongs of the forks, and handed them around.

All of them settled on fallen logs close to the campfire, Jack between Ashley and the ranger. "My sister always burns marshmallows," Jack told Ali.

"I do not!" Ashley cried.

"Maybe you just like the outsides all black and crusty," Jack teased. "Cremated marshmallows, Ashley's favorite kind. You ought to get some tiny little urns for them so they can rest in peace."

"Jack, let up," Steven warned, shooting him a look. "We have a guest. Ashley, you're such a great storyteller, why don't you tell us a campfire story?"

Ashley's expression was innocent enough, but Jack could hear the bite in her voice as she answered, "Let's let Jack do it. My brother, Jack, just loves to tell tales, especially to Mom and Dad."

"Really?" Ali asked. "I'd love to hear you tell a story, Jack. It's a perfect night for it, dark and quiet, with this nice campfire. Before Glacier became a national park, Native Americans probably sat around a campfire just like this one—maybe right on this same spot—telling tales about animals and hunting and brave deeds."

OK, Jack thought, Ashley's trying to make me look bad, but I'll show her. I'll fix her good. He leaned forward, trying to think up a story about animals and hunting and brave deeds. He began:

A long time ago, millions of buffalo lived on the plains, grazing on the sweet grass. Bands of nomads lived on the plains, too, sometimes following the herds of buffalo. They carried their buffalo-hide teepees with them and set up camp wherever they decided to stay for a while.

Hunters with bows and arrows would kill buffalo whenever they needed to, to provide food for their families. This was easy in the warm days of summer, but when winter was coming on, they needed extra meat to store up for the long, cold days of deep snow.

One of the hunters had a son and a daughter. "Son," he said, "this year you will help with the buffalo hunt."

The boy was only 12 years old. He knew that his arm was not strong enough to shoot an arrow through a thick buffalo hide. If he failed, he would be humiliated before his father and the others in the tribe. Still, he would never disobey his father—or his mother. If she told him not to do something, he always listened to her. He was a good son.

"This is what will happen," the father told him. "Two days from now, when the sun stands straight overhead at noon, you will put on the hide of a buffalo calf.

Then you will lead the herd over the edge of that cliff."
The father pointed to a precipice in the distance.

The boy's sister grew wide-eyed. She wasn't nearly as brave as her brother, but she liked to pretend that she was. "What can I do to help?" she asked in a small voice.

"You can move the rocks," her father told her.

The next day, the young girls and boys of the tribe began to pile rocks up high, making long, straight walls. These "drive lines" would lead the buffalo to the edge of the cliff. The sister worked hard, tugging rocks into place, but the brother didn't have to do this lowly chore because his job would be much more important. To practice for the great buffalo jump, he ran toward the cliff and leaped over, landing on a ledge beneath the edge of the precipice. He practiced again and again while his sister worked hard moving rocks. When all the rocks were stacked, the girl was so tired she went right to sleep inside the teepee.

The day of the hunt, the people of the tribe stood behind the herd of buffalo and started shouting, moving the big animals through the rock piles, running them toward the cliff. Some of the people wore wolf skins to frighten the buffalo to stampede through the drive lines. When the herd got close enough, the brave boy raced in front of the thundering herd, making noises like a buffalo calf. He knew that hunters would be waiting below the cliff with their bows and arrows ready. He hoped and prayed that none of the hunters would *think that the boy was a real buffalo and take aim at him as he leaped over the edge. But whatever happened, he would perform his duty with a strong, pure heart.*

With the herd at his heels, the boy jumped. He flew through the air, landing just where he was supposed to. Above his head, the buffalo plunged over the cliff. But the boy was not afraid.

More and more buffalo jumped, landing on top of one another on the ground below. Some of them lived to limp away, but most of them died. The ones that lived but were too hurt to run were killed.

Then, at the bottom of the cliff, the butchering began. The brave boy's sister had to cut meat from the bone and pull out the intestines, because the people used every part of the buffalo, even the eyes. That was his sister's main job—to pull out the eyes. But she was always so scared of things that she—

"Oh, puh-leeze!" Ashley shouted, jumping to her feet. Her eyes blazed, partly from the reflection of the fire, but mostly from sheer anger. "You're not funny, Jack, and you're a real jerk! That's absolutely the worst story I ever heard. It's not even a story!"

"Well,…I thought it was very original," Steven said.

Apologetically, Olivia explained to Ali, "We were at Ulm Pishkun this morning. I think Jack got carried away…."

Ali laughed and said, "I thought it was a great story.

Did you make that up all by yourself, Jack?"

Flushed with success, Jack answered, "Yeah, but I got a lot of the details from the exhibits at Ulm Pishkun. You know, like about the eyeballs. How about you, Ali? Can you tell us a story? Like, did you ever have a close encounter with a grizzly?"

"Yes. A very, very, *very* close encounter."

"Cool! Tell us." In the flickering light from the campfire, Jack was aware of his mother's frown, which meant that Jack was probably going to get into trouble for asking Ali to tell a story that would spook Ashley even worse. But, hey, she started it!

"Well," Ali began, "I was kind of new to this job and this park, and I went out hiking alone. That was my first mistake. It was late in August, up at Logan Pass, east of here."

Interrupting, Olivia suggested, "Ashley, why don't you come over and sit next to me?"

"I'm OK, Mom," she answered.

"So," Ali continued, "I sat down by a stream right in the middle of perfect grizzly habitat and started writing a letter. Later—I don't know how long it was— I looked up and there, about five feet away, was a grizzly slowly walking toward me."

"Wow!" Jack exclaimed. "What'd you do?"

"First my heart sank about down to my toes." Ali chuckled a little, remembering. "Then I said, 'Hey, bear,' very quietly. I knew enough not to run or to yell. You never, never, never try to run from a bear. If you do, it'll chase you, and no human being on Earth can out-run a bear."

Now it was Ashley who asked, very softly, "What happened?"

"I had taken my boots and my backpack off. They were resting next to me, so I just rolled over in the fetal position and kind of waited there, trying to get my heart to be quiet. I didn't hear anything from the bear, so I thought, OK, maybe he's gone. Behind me was a little stream, and I heard a splash, so I peeked under my arm. About ten feet back was the bear, with my back-pack under his chin. He was lying with his snout in my boot."

A bark of nervous laughter escaped from Ashley. "Your boot?"

"Uh-huh. I was watching him, and he looked over at me and kind of said with his eyes, 'Don't look at me,' so I looked back down. You're not supposed to make eye contact with bears. So I was lying there staring at the rock and thinking, well, maybe I can get away. I looked back at the bear again. Now he was chewing on my camera, and with his long claws, he had almost opened the part where you put the film in. Then once again he looked over as if to say 'Don't look at me,' but I kinda watched him, and he put the camera back in my bag, nice and neat, and stood up and started walk-ing toward me until he was right above me."

This time Ashley gasped, so engrossed she didn't even notice when her marshmallow oozed off the fork and plopped into the fire.

"He had his paw next to me, and I thought, OK, I've had a good life. I put my head back down. The grizzly sniffed down my back and then back up my back, and I kind of twitched my shoulder blade a bit, and then I felt a gentle nudge on my shoulder from the bear's snout. I waited for teeth or claws, but I didn't feel anything. Then I heard some bushes rustling up ahead of me. I looked up slowly, and saw a little tail on the back end of this big bear. He was walking away from me!"

Jack let out a breath. "Whew! Lucky you!"

Olivia said, "That was really unusual behavior. Normally, bears try to avoid people."

"So that was it? That's all that happened?" Ashley asked.

"Yep. The amazing thing was the bear didn't eat any of my food, and I had Oreos. He just left all my food untouched, fortunately, because they say, 'A fed bear is a dead bear.'" Ali paused, glancing down at the fire as she told them, "Once bears get people food, that's when they really begin to cause trouble. They start breaking into cabins and approaching people and cars. Luckily that bear didn't eat my food, so nothing was done to him." She looked up again, glad to let them know that her story had a happy ending.

"You mean, if he'd eaten your Oreos, something would have been done to him?" Ashley wanted to know.

"Uh-huh. We'd have targeted him."

Did that mean shoot him? To Jack, that sounded like a pretty severe penalty for eating a few cookies. *Bang!* At that precise second a branch snapped in the fire like a rifle shot, sending up a cascade of orange sparks into the night. Steven picked up a stick stirring the fire and spreading it out a bit so it wouldn't burn as high.

"We always hope we don't have to destroy them," Ali continued carefully. "Whatever we decide, it's an unpleasant process for the bears. Sometimes they get captured and relocated. We don't want bears to hurt people, or the other way around."

Hesitant, Ashley stammered, "I read...a book...."

"Night of the Grizzlies?" Ali smiled at Ashley. "Everybody seems to read that when they come to Glacier. It all happened a long, long time ago. Things were very different then. The park staff sort of...uh...looked the other way in those days if visitors fed the bears up at Granite Park Chalet. There was an open-pit garbage dump right near the chalet, so the bears would come around regularly. To the visitors, it was great entertainment, but it turned out to be disastrous. Now we require people to lock up their food or hang it high in trees at campsites so bears won't even try to get it. We also have Karelian bear dogs."

Olivia leaned forward. In the light from the campfire, her eyes reflected sudden animation. "I know about them," she said. "They were bred in Russia specifically to scare bears. Usually they stay on the leash and just bark at the bears to try to move them away from a people area."

"Right. And if you'd like to see a couple of Karelian bear dogs in action," Ali announced, "you're in luck. Two of their handlers from the Wind River Bear Institute happen to be in the park tomorrow to harass a bear we've been having problems with. It's a big male that keeps hanging out near a cabin. The dogs will try to teach it to stay back in the woods, away from people."

Olivia exclaimed, "Fantastic! The kids are coming with me tomorrow, and I know they'd love to see the dogs in action, too. Right, guys?"

"Yeah!" Jack and Ashley called out.

As the fire died down, Ali got up to leave, first brushing bits of leaves and bark from the back of her pants. "OK, Olivia, I'll pick up you and the kids at 8 a.m. Have a good night, folks. And thanks for the story, Jack. Maybe you'll be a writer someday."

CHAPTER FIVE

A mere five days had passed since the summer solstice, the time of year with the most hours of daylight, and the Landons happened to be camped less than 20 miles south of the Canadian border. That meant the sun rose even earlier than at their home in Jackson Hole, Wyoming, hundreds of miles farther south. These thoughts tugged at Jack's brain while he tried to decide whether to open his eyes. Even through his closed eyelids, he could tell that sunlight was sliding through the mesh-screen window next to his head. Could be 5:30, or as early as 5 a.m. To find out for sure, he'd have to open at least one of his eyes to look at his watch.

But why was the camping trailer moving?

Balanced on two tires and a jack beneath the trailer hitch, the trailer always teetered a little when anyone walked in it. Or—and this thought made Jack's eyes fly wide open—it could be a grizzly pawing the outside of the camper, getting ready to slash the canvas with six-inch claws!

Luckily, it didn't turn out to be anything that exciting—just Ashley, prowling around. Before Jack had a chance to ask her why she was up so early, she was gone, tiptoeing through the trailer door, closing it quietly behind her.

Probably she had to use the bathroom. She wasn't supposed to go even that short distance by herself because of a possible bear encounter, but last night, when he'd volunteered to accompany her down the path to the john, she'd practically hissed at him, "Leave me alone! I don't need you."

"So all right," he'd muttered then. "Go ahead and get eaten by a bear. You're the one who's so spooked about bears. Not me."

Now Jack yawned and looked at his watch. 5:12. At bedtime last night, he'd called the toss of a coin that let him win the queen-size bed, so Ashley had to sleep on the bench-with-a-mattress. But since his bed was right next to the unzipped window facing east, he was getting a full dose of sunrise. Sighing, he decided he might as well get up. Besides, he was curious about Ashley. Seven minutes had passed, and she wasn't back yet.

Trying not to rock the floor too much, he picked up his tennis shoes and crept outside, first noticing that his parents were still peacefully asleep.

Sitting on a tree stump, he pulled on his shoes but didn't bother tying them. His long legs, stretching up from the floppy shoelaces to the bottom hem of his sleep shirt, were tanned except for the tops where shorts usually covered them. In the early sunlight, his leg hair looked fuzzy and golden. Like his dad, Jack was a blond.

He walked along the path to the outdoor john and gently tapped on its metal door. "Ashley?"

No answer.

"If you're in there, answer me."

Nothing.

"Darn it, Ashley," Jack said, louder now, "don't joke around!"

From a distance, maybe as much as a hundred feet away in the tangle of Douglas fir and springy ground cover, he heard, "You don't have to wake up the whole world, Jack." Next came a rustling of leaves, and then, wading out through patches of wild roses like some forest sprite, Ashley appeared, fully dressed. When she stared at him, her expression was—there was no other way to say it—weird. Once again, weird.

"What the heck were you doing back in those trees?" Jack demanded.

"Oh, just enjoying the morning." She took a deep breath and smiled, but it didn't look anything like a real smile. "I've decided I don't want to go with Mom to park headquarters this morning. It's so pretty around here, I'll just stay at the campground."

"Fat chance," he scoffed. "Dad's taking a hike with his camera equipment to shoot pictures at that lake we passed on the way here. You think Mom's going to let you stay by yourself?"

"She might. If I tell her I can't stand to drive down that awful road and get carsick all over again. And"—Ashley deliberately sweetened her fake smile—"if my big brother offers to stay with me."

Jack narrowed his eyes. Something was definitely going on here, something only Ashley was aware of. Had she discovered a nest of baby animals of one kind or another? Ashley got all gooey over baby animals. If that was it, maybe Jack could get some really good pictures. As always, he'd brought his camera and plenty of film. "You found something, right?" he asked her.

She shrugged.

"Come on, tell me."

"As *if!* The last time I told you a secret—like, yesterday—you blabbed."

Jack grimaced. She was right. But his curiosity kept growing; he needed a way to persuade Ashley to spill it, whatever it was. "There's no guarantee Mom will leave us here even if I do stay with you," he said.

Ashley doubled over, clutching her middle. "Ooooh, I'm sick from all those burnt marshmallows last night. A car ride's gonna make it so much worse! I'm scared I'll throw up all over Ali's park vehicle."

What a little actress, Jack thought. But for Ashley to be willing to deliberately mislead their parents, the secret must be really big and important. She might not be as truthful, always, as her big brother, Jack the Eagle Scout, but she was pretty close to it. And whenever she did bend the truth a little, in her own mind it was usually justified by doing a good deed for some needy creature or person.

"If I agree to help you persuade Mom and Dad to leave us here, when do I find out what you're up to?" he asked her.

Now it was Ashley's turn to consider. She cocked her head, squinted one eye, and looked him over. Slowly, she said, "As soon as Mom and Dad leave. Deal?"

Jack raised his hand for a high five and said, "Deal!"

When they got back to the campsite, their mother was kneeling on the backseat of the Jeep with the door open, reaching into the tailgate. "You kids!" she said, sounding irritable.

"What?" Jack said.

"That game you play about who can close the car door more quietly? One of you left the door unlatched last night."

Olivia climbed out of the Jeep to confront them. "You know how important it is to have all the fresh food tightly sealed in a container and locked inside the vehicle. Bears can smell food a mile away."

"Yeah, I know but—" Jack began.

"So the door wasn't closed all the way," Olivia went on, "and some creature or other got inside. It must have been a raccoon, because I don't know any other animal with paws agile enough to open the catch on our cooler. But what if it had been a bear that got into our food! That would have been disastrous. Remember what Ali said—'A fed bear is a dead bear.'"

Meekly, Ashley murmured, "It was probably me who didn't close the car door all the way. Sorry, Mom. Did the raccoon take anything?"

"As far as I can tell," Olivia answered, "all that's missing is a couple of hot dogs."

"Should have taken some buns and mustard, too," Jack said, trying to be funny.

Olivia just glared at him. "From now on, you kids make sure these doors are tightly closed. Hear?"

Maybe it was just that Ashley happened to be standing in a shaft of sunlight that angled through heavy fronds of fir, but her cheeks looked pinker than usual.

"Gotcha, Mom," Jack answered.

She pulled it off, Ashley did. Their mother left with Ali, and their father—after being convinced that Ashley just needed to rest, and no, she didn't want her dad to stay—finally left on his photo-shoot hike. But before they said good-bye, Jack and Ashley were bombarded with instructions:

Steven: "You don't make a move alone. If one of you goes somewhere, the other goes, too."

Olivia: "The food stays in the cooler inside the Jeep. If you want any cheese or fruit or orange juice, get it out of the cooler but make sure you shut it. Garbage gets locked inside the Jeep, too."

Steven: "I won't be that far from here. Lake Winona is just across the road and a little way up—not more than a mile. If you want to come find me, I should be visible along the shoreline. Take the binoculars."

Olivia: "But unless there's an emergency, do not leave the area of the campground, hear? You can play in the creek, or go fishing if you want to, or play cards on the picnic table—"

Steven: "As soon as Ali and Mom leave, I'm going to lock the chain across the campground entrance so no other vehicle can turn in here."

Ashley had been staring solemnly at first one parent and then the other while the list of instructions went on and on—she looked like a spectator at a Ping-Pong match. Jack started to laugh.

His father's fingers dug hard into his shoulders. "Come here, young man!"

"What?"

Steven didn't answer as he marched Jack toward the entrance of the campground and stopped him in front of a red-and-white sign with a picture of a grizzly on it.

"Do you see that?"

"Yeah, I saw it before."

"Well, read it to me. Out loud."

Parents! With exaggerated patience, Jack read, "Bear Country. Bears Enter This Campground. Store All Food In Vehicle. All Wildlife Is Dangerous. Do Not Approach Or Feed."

"Well, remember it." Steven gave Jack an only halfway playful cuff on the back of the head.

At last Steven took off, his tripod and monopod sticking out of the straps on his backpack, making him look like an antenna-bristling, battery-operated toy. At the same time, with one final, worried frown, Olivia leaned forward from the front seat of the park vehicle to wave, as Ali started the motor. The two kids waved back, first at their mother, then at their father, smiling assurances at both parents as they went in opposite directions: Olivia south, Steven north.

"I thought they'd never go," Ashley breathed before the van had driven altogether out of sight. "Look, Mom's still waving through the back window."

"Yeah." A moment later, Jack declared, "I can't see either one of them now. The trees are hiding them. So!" He crossed his arms to confront Ashley. "I did my part of the deal. Now you have to let me in on your secret. What is it? Some helpless little animal in a nest?"

Ashley giggled. "You *could* say that."

"Then let's go see it. Only first, I want to get my camera out of the trailer."

Inside, the camping trailer was beginning to get stuffy. Jack unzipped all the clear plastic sheeting that covered the mesh screens on the windows, then lowered the metal panel on the upper half of the door. It was good to let in as much fresh air as possible; otherwise, by late afternoon, the trailer would be stifling. Shoving an extra roll of film into the pocket of his shorts, then hanging his camera around his neck by the strap, he opened the door and stepped outside.

Ashley was gone.

CHAPTER SIX

Jack stood stock-still in the center of the campsite. Nothing moved, not even the leaves on the wild roses that broke the monotony of green with the colorful splash of their vivid pink blossoms. He turned all the way around, first checking the Jeep parked beside the fir trees. She wasn't in there.

She wasn't sitting at the picnic table farther away in a little clearing, or next to the fire pit sunk in the ground. Probably she was playing mind games, trying to spook him. Maybe she'd hidden behind the brown-painted garbage can bolted to a concrete base. But unless she crouched in exactly the right spot in relation to his line of sight, the garbage can couldn't hide all of her. One little giveaway patch of red shorts would have been easy to see.

The creek, then, maybe. Their campsite was nicely located a hundred yards from the rushing waters of

Quartz Creek. Jack walked the distance to the creek, which was wide enough to wade across yet swift enough to splash and soak anyone who did. He looked up and down both banks. No Ashley.

No sense calling out for her beside the creek—its noise would drown out her reply, if she bothered to shout back. Whatever game she was playing, she probably wouldn't answer him anyway.

He went back to the trailer. Maybe she'd ducked back inside when he walked to the creek. But she hadn't. The beds were neatly made, all the boxed dried food was locked away, and the morning's dishes lay drying on the drain board.

Next, check the john. Maybe he'd meet her coming back from the john. But when he got there, everything was just as still as before.

The pump. Another hundred yards down the double tracks left by vehicles stood a green-painted pump, one of those with a handle that you pull up and down to get water—not for drinking, but for washing. Beside it was a flat concrete box of some kind sunk into the ground. It had a sheet metal lid; Jack lifted the lid to find another metal box inside the concrete, and inside that were metal pipes that had something to do with the pump. Ashley might have been able to squeeze inside there, if she were trying to hide from him. But except for the pipes, the box was empty.

Enough of this! He was beginning to get mad

now. "Ashley!" he yelled, "you better answer me."

He waited, straining to hear, and then her voice came from—he wasn't really sure where. "OK."

"Where are you? You know you're not allowed to go off all by yourself."

"I'm not all by myself."

"Huh?" Since he didn't know where to look, all he could do was keep shouting, "Get back here, Ashley! Now!"

Then, once again pushing through the leaves as she had early that morning, Ashley appeared. And not alone. By the hand, she led a boy, shorter than she was, but close to the same age.

Jack had the strange feeling that he might still be asleep and dreaming, or reliving his fantasy from Ulm Pishkun. The boy was the buffalo runner of Jack's fantasy. Brown skinned: His bare torso, arms, and face were the color of maple-sugar candy. Hair: thick, black, and tangled. Eyes: such a dark brown they looked almost black. But it was his bearing that reminded Jack of the buffalo runner—this boy didn't hang back; he kept pace with Ashley, not as someone being led, but as someone filled with confidence and curiosity, ready to take charge of any new situation. It didn't matter that his shorts were torn and dirty, or that his tennis shoes were ragged, or that his legs were scratched and he looked like he could use a good meal: This was a boy who knew who he was and what he wanted.

Now they were almost up to Jack. They stopped, both Ashley and the boy smiling. "Meet Miguel," Ashley said.

"Who...how...?" Jack sputtered.

"Our stowaway. He sneaked into our camping trailer when we stopped at the visitor center at Ulm Pishkun," Ashley explained.

"That's impossible," Jack protested. "No one could have got into that trailer when it was already folded down."

"Well, Miguel did. Can you imagine, Jack? He rode all those miles squished almost flat inside the trailer on that bumpy road that made *me* sick just sitting in the backseat of the Jeep. He's got to be pretty darn tough to have handled a ride like that."

"Wait a minute." Jack smacked his forehead. "That 'baby deer' you said you saw when we were setting up the trailer...."

"Uh-huh, it was Miguel." Ashley giggled. "That was when I was mad at you because you squealed to Mom about the book, so I wasn't going to tell you anything."

"I *knew* that wasn't any deer. So you were covering up all along. But what—who—"

Her smile got bigger; she was enjoying this, he could tell. "There's a big piece of the puzzle you're missing. Think a minute. When we left Ulm Pishkun...in the car...." She waited, challenging him to figure it out.

What did she mean? Jack frowned, forcing his mind

to go over everything that had happened since they left Ulm Pishkun, trying to visualize it like a videotape running backward.

"The newspaper…," Ashley hinted.

Suddenly he got it. "He's the Mexican kid they wrote about!" Jack exclaimed. "The one who sneaked across the border all by himself. Three times!"

"Bingo," Ashley said quietly, and raised Miguel's hand, which she was still holding, lifting it up like he was a champ.

Through all this talk Miguel had been peering from Jack to Ashley, back and forth, his eyes bright and interested, his expression curious.

"You've got to be kidding. This is him?"

"Yep."

"Can he talk?" Jack asked.

Ashley turned to Miguel. "This is my brother, Jack, I told you about," she said. "He wants to know if you can talk. Say something to him."

Miguel grinned, his teeth large and white in his brown face. "Hey, dude," he said.

It was so unexpected that Jack burst out laughing. "Hey *dude?* You know English!"

"Ummmmm, *un poco,*" Miguel nodded, holding his thumb and forefinger close together. "Little bit."

"Miguel told me all about his escape from Mexico," Ashley said. "That's why I had to sneak out and meet him this morning. All last night you wouldn't let me go anywhere alone for more than five minutes."

"That was because of the bears," Jack said, trying to remember what had seemed so important about their feud less than 12 hours before. Nothing much, he realized.

"Forget bears. This," Ashley said, wiggling her eyebrows, "is bigger than bears. This is rescuing somebody who needs us. Are you going to help?"

Jack didn't know what to say. Standing there, in the sun-dappled clearing, it seemed impossible that he was actually in front of a Mexican runaway, one who had been reported in the papers and who was even now probably being hunted by the police. Even more impossible was the fact that his sister had managed to keep a secret this big from both his parents and him. All he could think to say was, "You must be hungry, right, Miguel?" He tried to remember any shred of Spanish he'd learned in school, but the only words that came to mind were *sí* and *no,* and those weren't going to get him very far. "Hungry," Jack said again, bringing his fingers up to his lips as if he were taking a bite. Again, more slowly, he said, "Eat. Food."

"He's not deaf, Jack."

Miguel nodded, patting his flat stomach. The sound it made was as hollow as a stick beating a drum. *"Sí,* eat. Food. *Bueno."*

"Last night I told him how to get into the Jeep and take the hot dogs," Ashley said, "but I bet he's starving now. Come on, Miguel." Tugging his arm, she pulled him in the direction of the trailer, calling to Jack over her shoulder, "He's on his way to Seattle to be with a teacher who used to live in Mexico. He says he wants to work in her restaurant."

Miguel turned to smile broadly, eyes bright, dark hair standing in stiff tufts that looked like black feathers. "I go Seattle," he said haltingly. "Earn money."

"But he's too young! How can he—"

"Food first," Ashley told Jack, "then the story."

Every time Miguel emptied the green plastic bowl of Cheerios Ashley had given him, she poured more into it, as if it were bottomless. Miguel wolfed the food so quickly, bits of milk dribbled down his chin. Periodically he'd stop to wipe his mouth with the back of his hand, then return to the cereal with an intensity Jack had never seen before.

Ashley sat cross-legged at Miguel's elbow, pouring milk into the bowl to keep it filled. Jack had settled in across from them, watching, thinking, wondering what to do next. How would it feel to be that hungry? Jack always felt deprived if he missed a snack before bedtime, and here was this little kid, who had traveled from another country without a dime and no food at all, who looked dirty and bug bitten and road weary. It reminded Jack once again why his dad welcomed foster kids into their home whenever they got a call from the Jackson, Wyoming, Social Services. "Being a foster kid myself, I came through some hard times," Steven had often told Ashley and Jack. "I want to help kids who are in the same rough place I was."

Miguel ate until the box rattled empty and his stomach bulged, round and hard. Finally satisfied, he settled back contentedly, his smile wide and lopsided. *"Gracias,"* he told them.

"You're welcome," Jack answered. Then, to Ashley, "Now what?"

"Miguel, tell Jack what happened to you. Tell him why you are here."

Nodding solemnly, Miguel began his story. "I come from Nogales, near the border. Shantytown, no water, my sister carry *agua* from the river. My—*familia*—live in house of paper."

"Paper?" Jack asked.

"I think he means cardboard," Ashley explained.

"We want to work, but no work. No work, no *pesos.* I always dream to come to the other side." He said all this as though he'd recited it often, maybe to get food from sympathetic listeners on his journeys.

" 'The other side' means the United States," Ashley told Jack. "Go on, Miguel, tell Jack where you're going."

Miguel took a deep breath and concentrated, trying to make the words come out right: *"Hace mucho tiempo*—a long time ago—maybe six years—*seis años*— my brother have a teacher, Crecensia Álvarez. She hate to see children go hungry. She want better life for her people. So she come to U.S.A. to sell burritos, tacos, enchiladas—real food from Mexico, with spice hot like fire. *Norteamericanos* love her food. Now she is rich, with many *restaurantes*. She give always a job to people from Nogales." Jabbing a finger into his chest, Miguel announced, "I will work for *Señora* Álvarez. Send money to my family."

"Work! How old are you?" Jack asked.

"Ten," Miguel answered. "Old enough."

"You want to work when you're only ten? What about school?"

Miguel shrugged. *"No es importante."*

"Sure it is," Jack exploded. "Anyway, you can't get a job if you're only ten."

Miguel laughed and held up the fingers of both hands. "I work when I was this many—*ocho años.* Eight. In *supermercado.* I carry groceries to cars. No pay; tips only."

Ashley looked at Miguel with admiration. "Go on, Miguel, tell Jack how you left Mexico and got all the way to Montana," she encouraged.

Grinning, he answered, "I ride the rails."

"He hopped a train, Jack. Can you believe it? He said he sneaks onto trains all by himself. He's done it a lot—that's how he learned English, 'cause usually the trains took him to Texas or California, and when he'd get there he'd hang out with a bunch of other home-less people till he got caught. But it hasn't always been good. One time some hobos stole his shoes."

"*Sí*. My shoes got swipe," Miguel said, wiggling his toes. When he noticed Jack staring at the toenails protruding through the holes in the dirty canvas, Miguel added, "These I find in garbage can in San Diego."

"And each time the immigration officials caught him, they sent him right back. I think it's wrong that the U.S. does that to him, don't you? Miguel's just trying to help his family, but nobody cares, so they make him go home to his paper house in Nogales."

"Then he's been caught—"

"Two times—once in Sacramento, California, and once in Salt Lake City. But this time he's made it all the way to Montana. He's been sneaking into trucks, and when one of them stopped at Ulm Pishkun, he got out. Then he saw a man in uniform and thought it was a policeman—it was probably a park ranger—so he opened the bottom part of our trailer door and ducked inside. Before he could get out, we started driving."

Miguel sat there nodding, although he probably couldn't follow much of what Ashley was saying.

"He's lucky we were heading west," she added. "He's been trying every way he could to make it to Seattle."

"*Sí*. To find *Señora* Álvarez," Miguel said.

Ashley questioned Jack with her dark eyes. "Are you going to tell Mom and Dad?"

"I—I don't know."

"Jack! You *promised!* You said I could trust you. If you tell, they'll *have* to call the police. Immigration officers will take him, after he's made it all this way. They'll send him back to Nogales. Is that what you want? Do you want him to live where there's no electricity and not enough food?"

Jack could answer this one honestly. "No," he said, "I don't want that at all." Still, he didn't like the idea of lying to his parents, and they'd have to do a lot of lying to keep Miguel a secret. He studied the boy, who had once again picked up the plastic bowl. "Just what do you want to do with him, Ashley? We can't keep him here. He's not a pet."

"Don't you think I know that?"

"Then what's your plan?"

"I haven't gotten that far yet," she admitted, "to have a plan." Fanning her face with her hand, she added, "Oooh, it's hot in here." Her skin was flushed, and Jack could see bits of perspiration glistening where her hair framed her face. Jumping to her feet, she flung open the door of the trailer as far as it would go, then stood next to Jack. Bending close, using an exaggerated whisper, she said, "For starters, maybe it would be a good idea to give him a bath. He kind of…smells."

"Smell?" Miguel asked before he tipped the bowl and drained the last drops of milk.

"*Sí, poco,*" Ashley answered, smiling apologetically at Miguel. "Let's grab some shampoo and head to the creek. While we're scrubbing, maybe we can figure out what to do next. Jack, do you have any extra clothes that will fit him?"

"Nothing his size. He's littler than you. What do you have?"

"A Utah Jazz T-shirt, which I love, but I guess it'll have to do, since everything else I packed would look too girly on him." Sighing, she rummaged through her duffel bag and brought out a faded purple and gray shirt, and then a pair of black shorts. Elbow deep, she poked around until she pulled up a pair of sandals, the kind with Velcro fasteners. "These might work, too," she said.

"Mom bought those for you for this trip, and they cost 50 bucks!" Jack objected.

"So? I have other shoes. Miguel's got nothing. We shouldn't be pigs, Jack."

"Pig?" Miguel repeated, looking puzzled. "Ah, *puerco!*" He laughed, then patted his stomach and burped, making Jack and Ashley laugh with him.

CHAPTER SEVEN

White angelica next to Quartz Creek bloomed like soap bubbles on green straws, nodding to the water as it rushed on its way to Lower and Middle Quartz Lakes. Though it swirled with foamy ripples, the water didn't look too deep, especially where it pooled behind a string of boulders polished smooth by the swift current. Branches and bits of sticks had lodged against the stones, damming the water into a small pool. A perfect bathing spot.

"There," Ashley said, pointing. "That's where we'll clean him. It'll be cold, but it's the best we can do, 'cause I don't have a clue how to rig up that shower bag thing Dad has. You ready, Jack?"

"I guess. I'm not sure Miguel understands what we're doing here."

"Sure he does, don't you, Miguel?" Miguel shrugged and smiled, a sign Ashley took for "yes" but that Jack interpreted as "I have no idea." Both he and Ashley were in their bathing suits, so Miguel most likely just figured they were going in for a swim. Jack looked away from Miguel's trusting eyes. Poor guy was really in for it now.

"OK, Jack, I'll turn my back while you tell him to get undressed. Tell him to leave his underwear on, though," Ashley instructed.

"You do it."

"I'm not going to. That's a guy thing. After you get him in, I'll give his hair a really good shampoo."

Jack snorted. "Give us a break. Miguel can wash his own hair."

"Not as well as I can," came her reply. "You don't mind me washing your hair, do you, Miguel?"

Another shrug, another grin.

"There you go, Jack, he's fine with it." Ashley had armed herself with a full load of supplies, from biodegradable shampoo to biodegradable soap to fresh underwear (Jack's), her own Jazz T-shirt and black shorts, a spare toothbrush and toothpaste, comb and scissors, and her sandals, all of which she'd loaded into a clean plastic garbage bag and slung over her shoulder.

They seemed like mother and child, Ashley and Miguel, which amused Jack because the two of them were exactly the same age.

"All right, I'll wait up on the bank," Ashley told him. "You get him in the water and then call me."

Jack asked, "You sure you want to do this?"

"Sure I'm sure. He stinks. Besides, I want to cut his hair after it's wet—"

"No way," Jack protested. "The only hair you've ever cut was on your Barbie dolls."

"They looked great!"

"They were *bald!*"

"Only Malibu Barbie. Besides, that was a long time ago. Come on, Jack, it'll only be a trim! I'll just snip a teeny tiny bit, and he'll look a whole lot better." Supremely confident, she retreated up the bank of the creek to wait. Bushes rustled behind her, and then, like a forest animal disappearing into the underbrush, she was gone.

Jack turned to face Miguel, who was studying him with his large, dark eyes. "OK," Jack began, feeling completely stupid. "See the water? We want to go in. To wash." He scrubbed his fingers through his hair and pointed once again to the stream.

"*Sí.* Wash." Miguel seemed to have understood enough to act amused. They exchanged a look of "she's a girl—what can you expect?"

"So, you need to take off your clothes. But leave on your underwear," Jack added quickly. In a flash, Miguel kicked off his tattered sneakers, then scrambled out of his shorts and began to wade into the water. From behind, Jack saw that Miguel was completely naked. "Ashley," Jack sputtered, "stay up on the bank.

Whatever you do, don't come down here!"

"But I want to—"

"Miguel doesn't *have* any underwear."

"Oh," her voice floated down. "Never mind."

Great, Jack muttered. Now he was going to be the one responsible for following through with Ashley's idea. Well, there was no way he was going to scrub another guy, no matter how bad the other guy smelled. Yanking open the bag, Jack rooted around until he found the shampoo, soap, and a washcloth. When he waded in, his breath was caught by the coldness of the stream, until he let out a loud yelp and chattered, "Man, this is cold." Miguel didn't seem to mind it. Laughing loudly, he splashed the water with his palm, spraying Jack with an arc that caught the light in rainbow crystals.

"Oh, so you want to play rough, huh?" With his fist, Jack hit the water, returning fire, and as the battle escalated, both of them slipped on the algae-covered stones and fell flat in the stream. Laughing, sputtering out mouthfuls of creek, they kept up the water fight until they were thoroughly soaked. With hair plastered flat against their foreheads in wet stripes—Miguel's black, Jack's honey blond—they signaled each other: Truce!

Miguel then grabbed the shampoo and soap and cleaned himself until his brown skin was as smooth as a seal's.

"Ashley," Jack yelled, "we need towels. Bring that

big blue beach towel and leave it up behind those bushes that have the pink flowers."

"OK, but it'll take me a minute," she called back. "Last night I gave the blue beach towel to Miguel."

"You did? Why?"

"Because he needed something to keep him warm, and Mom would have noticed if I'd pinched one of the blankets. Hang on—I'll run back for it."

Jack felt a hint of worry. Their parents had told them to stay together when they went anywhere, especially into the woods, yet Ashley seemed to be going off by herself constantly without coming to any harm. In a few minutes she returned, the blue towel trailing behind her shoulders like Batman's cape. "Don't worry," she said, taking a halting step forward. "I'm looking only at the ground."

"Leave it on that bush. Good. Now, go away."

"Hurry up. I didn't mean for you and Miguel to have all the fun."

Back on the bank Miguel rubbed himself dry and dressed in the clothes Ashley had brought. Clean, dry, and sweet smelling, Miguel was a good-looking—dude. He seemed pleased as well. Rolling his old clothes into a ball, he was about to toss them into the creek when Jack stopped him. "No, this will go into the garbage," Jack instructed, taking the bundle and jamming it into the plastic bag. "Don't litter." He launched into a short lecture about keeping the park clean, about why they'd needed to use biodegradable soap and shampoo to protect the environment—but after watching Miguel's eyes glaze, he gave up. Jack had never realized how hard it was to get ideas across when there was no common language to build on.

"*Now* can I come down?" Ashley's voice drifted from somewhere near the picnic table. "I want to give him his haircut."

Jack groaned. "She wants to—" With his index and third finger, he made snipping motions to his own hair.

At first Miguel looked alarmed, but then he gave one of his shrugs—this time without the grin—and said, "*Sí*. OK."

When Ashley reached them, Miguel sat on a big rock, his back ramrod stiff, as if the slightest movement might result in decapitation. With the big blue towel wrapped around him to his feet, Miguel looked as small as an eight-year-old. "Now, don't move," Ashley warned. "Don't even breathe."

The haircut was not making Miguel especially happy, but maybe he felt he owed Ashley. Frowning in concentration, peering close, then standing back, she worked her way around Miguel, scissors winking in the bright sun. *Snip, snip, snip,* went the blades as bits of black hair fluttered to the ground. Bugs buzzed around, but Ashley ignored them, intent on her work. "OK…I think you're done."

She surprised Jack. She did a reasonably good job

on Miguel. "Not bad," she cried, brushing his neck. "There, Jack. *Now* try to tell me I can't cut hair." Looking speculatively at her brother, she raised the scissors and took a step in his direction.

"Not me!" he yelled, backing away from her. "Not ever! Forget it!"

"OK, OK, I'll just have to wait till you're asleep," she agreed cheerfully.

"Ashley!"

"Just kidding. Let's all go up to the picnic table and sit there while we figure out what to do. First I'll get dressed, then I'll get us some cans of soda—you want grape or orange or cola?"

The way Ashley was taking charge was a little much, but if Miguel could take it, Jack guessed he could, too. After he'd changed out of his bathing suit, they settled themselves at the picnic table—Jack and Miguel on one side, like the troops; Ashley on the other, like the general. Jack thought, I don't ever want to live in a world run by girls. But he kept quiet because he was curious to hear what Ashley was hatching in her little pea brain.

"I've wanted to keep Miguel a secret because Mom and Dad will have to call Social Services, and the officers will take Miguel away and send him back to Mexico, like they did the other two times."

When Miguel heard the word Mexico, his face clouded. "No Mexico," he told them.

"But how long can we keep a secret like this?" Jack protested.

"That's just it. Maybe we don't need to keep Miguel a secret any longer because I've been thinking," she announced. Obviously, while Jack and Miguel were in the creek, she'd been constructing a whole scenario of her own. "I'm figuring this: When Mom and Dad see Miguel, especially now that he looks so nice with that *great* haircut, they'll think he's cute."

"And your point is…?" Jack asked.

"Well, you know how we take in foster kids?"

Oh, wonderful, Jack thought. The one vacation we've had without a foster kid tagging along, and she wants to pick up one on the road. Out loud he said, "Ashley, that won't work. No matter what you're cooking up, he's still an illegal alien. He can't be a foster kid in the Social Services system if he's illegal. They'll have to send him back."

"Back? Nogales? No!" Miguel shook his head.

"I don't want Miguel as a foster kid," she said impatiently. "This is my idea: We'll *adopt* him! Then he'll be a U.S. citizen. He couldn't be sent away."

Jack sat in stunned silence.

"Listen, I've figured it all out. He'll sleep in the extra bedroom in our house where the foster kids usually stay, and when school starts in the fall, he'll go with me on the bus, because this year you'll be in junior high, Jack, so we won't be taking the same bus. I don't suppose Miguel will be put in my grade until he learns to speak English better, but he's smart, and I'll help him learn, so I bet by the end of the year—"

"Ashley!" Jack yelled to stop her.

"What?"

"You can't decide everything for everybody. Maybe Miguel doesn't want to live with us."

"Who wouldn't want to?"

"Me, sometimes!"

"What are you talking about?" Ashley looked at him with her chin thrust out stubbornly.

"Look, it's one thing to give someone a haircut when they don't want one, but it's a whole different thing to boss them on how they're going to live the rest of their lives. You can't just take over people, Ashley. You gotta stop this—hey, are you listening to me? I'm trying to talk to you."

"Shhh. Wait a second. Did you hear that?" Ashley held up her hand, motioning for Jack to be quiet. Looking toward the woods, she peered intently into the distance, her eyes narrowed.

"Come on, Ashley—"

"No! I mean it! Listen!"

Jack strained, but he heard nothing except the chirping of birds and the rustling of the wind through the treetops. "It's just the wind."

"No, there it is again. I can just barely hear. Way off, it's like a thumping. *Boom, boom, boom.*"

"Are you trying to psych me out?"

Ashley shook her head. "It's really soft…like…I don't know…a heartbeat." Tilting her head, she asked, "Didn't you hear that?"

The tiny hairs on the back of Jack's neck stood up when he heard the sound—a soft thumping in the distance, as if the air itself were pulsating. From the direction, he guessed it was coming from an area on the farthest edge of Quartz Creek Loop, maybe a quarter of a mile from their campsite. Whoever it was, they were back in the trees, well hidden from the Landon camp.

"I don't get it. No one is supposed to be in here," Jack said. "The entrance into Quartz Creek Campground is chained. This whole area is closed."

"Well, *somebody's* in the woods," Ashley shot back. "It sounds like music."

"The only other people who could possibly be back there are rangers. Or hikers."

"Maybe. I just hope it's not…." Ashley's face clouded. She bit her lip and looked at Miguel.

"What?"

Mouthing the words, so that she barely made a sound, Ashley whispered, "The police!"

Miguel must have been able to read lips. He jumped forward so fast Jack barely had time to grab his arm. "*¡Policía! ¡Policía!*" Miguel exploded.

"Hold on, Miguel, don't listen to Ashley—she's just

crazy. *¡Loco!* There's *no* police!"

"No Nogales! No!" Miguel cried, tugging at Jack's arm. For someone so small, Miguel was amazingly strong. It took all of Jack's strength to hold him.

"Way to go, Ashley," Jack hissed at his sister. "You've got him all freaked!"

"I was just thinking about the newspaper. They said the police were looking for him."

"Police don't crank up music in their patrol cars in the middle of the woods. Now Miguel believes he's about to be deported. Nice going!" Then, to Miguel, "Calm down. Listen to me, you're OK."

Miguel stared at Jack, his eyes round with panic, his breathing shallow.

"No police, Miguel. No worries. It's just hikers." He moved his index and third finger through the air as if they were walking. "Hikers. *¿Sí?*"

Suddenly, as abruptly as it started, the music stopped. The woods around them were silent once again, as if a giant plug had been pulled. A beat later it blared once again, only to be silenced just as quickly. The three of them stared at each other until Jack whispered, "Weird."

"We ought to check it out," Ashley said. "I have a great sense of direction, and I know I can take us right to where that music was coming from. But we won't go all the way there. We'll get Dad's binoculars so we can spy on them through the trees."

"Spy on *who?*"

"Whoever's out there playing that loud music. If we use the binoculars, we don't have to get too close, just in case it really is—uh—the *P* word."

Luckily, Miguel didn't panic this time because he didn't connect "the *P* word" to "police."

Jack was about to remind his sister that they weren't supposed to stray from their campground, but he was a little curious, too, about who might be out there in the woods.

"OK," he told Ashley. "Go get the binoculars."

The sun had long since burned off the early morning mist, and now the noon sky beat down in a stifling wave of heat. As they waited for Ashley, Jack and Miguel stayed at the picnic bench, huddled at the end where tree shadows offered shelter. Miguel's fingers picked tiny splinters from the wooden tabletop; every few seconds, he scanned the trees, watching for any movement, and then, like curtains being shut, his lids would drop down again. He looked scared, Jack thought. And why not? If Jack and Ashley couldn't make sense of the strange sounds, what must Miguel be thinking?

"Come on, Ashley," Jack called. "Hurry up."

"I'm trying. Just hold on—I can't find them."

"Dad said he left them in the trailer."

"I know, but he didn't say where. Give me a second."

Flies punctuated the stillness as they buzzed around the picnic table. *"Ashley, come on!"* Jack yelled impatiently.

"I give up," she said, emerging from the trailer. "They're not in there. Dad must have taken them with him by mistake."

"Great. No binoculars. Now what?"

"Well, I was thinking that if we hike up to the top of the loop in the road, maybe we could see who's back there," Ashley answered. "There's a lot of trees to hide behind."

"Ummm, I don't think so," Jack told her, shaking his head. "That's pretty far away, and we're supposed to stay right here in our own campground. If Mom and Dad found out we left here, we'd be grounded for life. Spying with binoculars from far away is one thing, but—"

"It's not that far! Look at Miguel, he's afraid the you-know-who are going to arrest him, which is my fault for bringing it up in the first place. I know that was dumb, but he's still scared. Don't you want to show him it's safe?"

Jack looked at Miguel, whose eyes flicked back and forth from Jack to Ashley to the road.

Weakening, Jack countered, "Maybe we ought to wait until Mom and Dad get back."

"By then whoever is doing whatever they're doing might be gone! Come on, Jack, we'll be like spies. We'll find them, we'll watch, we'll leave. Do it for Miguel if you won't do it for me."

That convinced him. "OK, but you have to do

exactly what I tell you, and go back when I tell you to, no questions asked."

"Absolutely!" Ashley agreed.

"All of us need to stay close and keep quiet. *Shhh,*" he told Miguel, his finger to his mouth.

Miguel had barely taken three steps from the picnic bench before he fell, sprawling in the dust. "Shoes too big," he said, kicking off Ashley's sandals. He went to where Jack had left the garbage bag to retrieve his old, torn sneakers.

"No, they're too dirty," Ashley protested.

"I think he wants to be able to run if he needs to."

"Well, if he has to wear those nasty shoes, then at least I'm going to scrape some of the dirt off." Ashley snatched the shoes from Miguel before he could sit down to put them on. "I'll take them to that green pump over there and squirt water on them. That'll help."

"He doesn't care about the dirt," Jack protested, but Ashley had already reached the pump and was pulling on the handle, lifting it and then shoving it down, again and again, until water began to gurgle and then came pouring through the spout. She held the sneakers on their sides beneath the rush of water, pumping the handle continuously. If the cloth in the sneakers didn't look much better, at least all the mud was being washed off the soles.

Miguel stood on the metal door that lay like a lid over the concrete compartment sunk coffinlike into the ground next to the pump. *"¿Qué es?"* he asked, lifting the lid and pointing to the pipes inside.

In answer, Jack showed him the small red sign on the front of the pump. "It says 'Notice, this water is treated with iodine.' I guess those pipes are part of the…." How was he supposed to explain the process of iodization to Miguel, when he couldn't even get him to understand that the police in the United States didn't go into closed campgrounds and crank up rock music to catch illegal aliens? He could sign the basics to Miguel, like food or a haircut, but ideas were something else. He needed words. Words that he didn't have. The whole thing was so frustrating! "Uh, the pipes put stuff in the water, that's all."

"Give it up, Jack, he doesn't understand a thing you're saying. Here you go, Miguel," Ashley interrupted, holding out the dripping sneakers.

"Good show, Ashley," Jack said. "Now every step he takes, he'll squish."

"But if he tries to run away from us, he might go slower." She nodded at Jack, a small smile curling the edge of her lips.

Jack answered with a grin. Sometimes his sister could be pretty smart.

CHAPTER EIGHT

Ashley in front, Jack in back, with Miguel in the middle, they hiked down a lane with two dirt tire tracks running in dusty parallel strips. The road through Quartz Creek Campground was shaped like a lasso, a straight stretch topped by a gigantic loop. The Landon camper was parked on the left side of the lasso; the sound seemed to have come from the farthest edge of the right side of the loop. Whoever they found would be too far back to know anyone else was in the campground.

Stopping abruptly, Ashley asked, "Ooooh, do you smell that awful smell?" Wrinkling her nose, she said, "It's like something really rotten."

Jack hadn't noticed it before, but once Ashley mentioned it, he could smell it, too, especially when a small breeze wafted toward them. "I don't know what it is," he answered, "but this whole thing is getting strange." Maybe the mystery would be solved when they got a look at who or what was back there in the trees. Or maybe it wouldn't turn out to be much of a mystery: Probably hikers had come in from the back country, not needing to unlock the chain at the entrance.

The farther they walked, the worse the smell became. With every breeze, a fresh wave of stench would curl up Jack's nostrils, as if death itself were riding the wind.

It didn't seem to bother Miguel, though. Nothing, it seemed, bothered him, not the rough ride in the camper, not the lack of food, not his dirty clothes, not anything except the police, whom he had good reason to fear, and even that danger he was prepared to face. With his frayed shoes and borrowed clothes, Miguel was at ease in his own skin. That kid, Jack mused, could teach him a lot.

Suddenly Miguel grabbed at Ashley's arm and motioned for Jack to stop. *"Por allí,"* he whispered, pointing. "There."

"What?" Jack hadn't noticed anything, not the slightest movement or flash of color.

Miguel pointed, then repeated, *"Por allí."*

"OK, I'll go first. You guys follow," Jack instructed.

"No," Miguel said. "I go first."

He must want to see if the police are there, Jack thought, as Miguel cut off the path and moved into the woods. After a hundred more feet, he started ducking behind tree trunks, one at a time, slowly and softly moving forward, nothing more than a shadow. Ashley and Jack followed, doing exactly what Miguel did. Underbrush thickened, scraping Jack's skin. Twigs snapped underfoot. The mysterious smell grew nauseating.

When they reached an opening, Miguel dropped to his belly and pointed. At first Jack could see nothing, but as he strained forward he made out the shape of a delivery van—dark green and inconspicuous in the midst of all the foliage. Jack motioned for his sister to stay down. Ashley made herself small, her eyes barely clearing the tall grass.

"That's not the police," Jack whispered to Miguel. "Look at the license plate. They're from Washington State, where Seattle is. No *policía*."

"*Sí*." Miguel nodded, growing tense.

The tension had nothing to do with Miguel's concern about police. Devouring the scene in front of him, he stared fiercely, hardly breathing, and Jack knew why. Miguel had heard the magic word *Seattle*. Jack followed his gaze.

Two men sat on folding chairs half hidden by a cluster of bushes, casually talking as though they were merely enjoying a vacation in the woods.

"Man, this silence is killin' me," one moaned.

"Then next time, moron, remember your headphones. You touch that stereo one more time, and I'll break your hand off."

"No one's even out here, Terry. What's the big deal?

You think maybe a squirrel's gonna report me? I hate nature—it's too quiet. Drives me crazy!"

"Will you stop with the music already? You're just antsy 'cause it's taking a lot longer this time," said the man called Terry, who sat with his left ankle perched on his right knee. He wore wraparound sunglasses, the metallic kind that made it impossible for his eyes to be seen. A Greek fisherman's hat tilted down so far that its brim touched the top of the sunglasses. His body seemed strong and athletic, but his mouth looked hard.

"I know it. I was thinkin' maybe the wind's blowing in the wrong direction," the other man said. "But you'd figure with that rotten deer over there, you wouldn't need to depend on a breeze to carry the smell. Whoo, that baby is ripe." He slapped his knee, maybe for emphasis, maybe hitting a bug. He was bareheaded, with no sunglasses, and young, about mid-20s, with long, reddish hair so curly it was almost fuzzy. He wore a muscle shirt that might have been white once but was now a dingy gray. His shoulder—the one facing Jack's direction—was crowded with tattoos.

Holding her hand over her nose, Ashley pointed past the men to the bloated carcass of a deer, a hundred yards from where the men sat. Why didn't they move away from that awful smell? It was bad enough to make Jack gag, and the two men were closer to it than he was. What was going on here? Maybe they ought to leave before they were spotted. Silently motioning to

Miguel and Ashley, Jack began to back slowly through the trees.

"Hey Max, did you hear something?" asked Terry, the man in the hat.

Had they been seen? Jack, Ashley, and Miguel froze, hardly breathing. Jack's heart began to bang in his chest. Every muscle stiffened.

"Yeah! Maybe this is it," Max answered quietly. "It's coming through on the left! I hope it ain't a big male. Give us a sow with three cubs."

Jack's breath escaped in a puff. They hadn't been seen. The men were looking off into the woods to the east of them.

"Yeah—that'd be luck," Terry agreed. "I'd settle for two cubs. Two'd be lucky. That'd earn a K for you and a K for me."

K? Did they mean a thousand? Dollars? For what? Jack reversed himself and crowded closer.

"Maybe we oughta move back even farther so it can't see us," Max murmured.

"We're pretty much hidden, but OK." Both men faded backward into the trees, not more than ten yards from where the kids lay hidden. Now the sound of rustling grew louder. Twigs snapped and popped. Something big was coming, cracking branches, shifting leaves.

"Got the gun?" Max asked softly.

"Ready and loaded. Come on, bear," Terry said, his

voice hushed. "Come get your lunch. Thatagirl."

A grizzly head appeared, weaving from side to side, the snout working as the adult female sniffed the air. One cub tried to push ahead of her; she swatted it back. A second cub stood unmoving near her back feet.

"Score," Max declared. "Two cubs."

Jack drew in his breath. In spite of the thick foliage, he could tell that Terry had raised a gun to his shoulder. They were going to kill the mother grizzly! Should he yell? Warn the bear? Reveal their position and take their chances? He twisted his head toward Ashley. His sister's skin had blanched white, and her eyes were wide with terror as she gripped Jack's arm. "It's a *grizzly!*" she mouthed.

"Let her get closer to the bait," Max said softly. "Bring her out of the woods into the clearing so I can get a better shot at the cubs."

They were going to kill the cubs, too!

The stench of rotting was so overpowering that in no way could the big grizzly have smelled humans nearby. If she heard them, she gave no sign. Unafraid, she lumbered toward the deer carcass on the ground. A trap to lure bears to their death!

Miguel scooted forward, taking in everything. Jack felt paralyzed. Choices whirled though his mind, all of them bad. He waited helplessly as the mother grizzly sank her teeth into the carcass. She was dark brown, thick furred, and healthy looking. One of the cubs had the same dark brown fur as the mother, like molasses; the other was lighter, more honey colored. The babies took timid bites.

"OK, let 'er rip," Max said, and before Jack could react, a shot rang out, but it didn't sound like a rifle shot; it was muffled, and the big grizzly didn't fall. She just stood there, on all fours, shaking her head as though annoyed, then trying to reach back to grasp, with her teeth, the metal tube that stuck out from her shoulder.

"Did you put in a big enough dose?" Max asked.

"Plenty."

"Then why isn't she falling down?"

"Sometimes it just takes longer," Terry answered. "Look, there she goes. Her front legs are buckling. Hurry up and dart the two cubs before they run."

But the cubs weren't making any attempt to leave. As the female bear slowly rolled on her side, grunting and twitching, her cubs nudged her with their snouts, unsure what had happened to their mother, not knowing what to do.

"Careful you don't hit big mamma again when you shoot the cubs," Max said.

"Here, you do it," Terry answered, handing Max the dart gun. "Use enough stuff in the darts to knock 'em out for a while."

Now Jack began to put the pieces together. These guys weren't planning to kill the mother bear or the cubs. They were poachers, out to steal them! So this was what had been happening to Glacier's yearling bears. His mother had thought the lack of cubs might be caused by a shortage of food in a drought year, or an unknown disease, or who knew what else? And all along, the bear cubs were being poached from the park.

Ashley stirred in the grass, tugging Jack's arm again, still looking terrified.

"*Shhh,* you'll be OK," Jack whispered. "The bear's tranquilized."

Max moved around for a better shot at the cubs, who were whimpering and nosing their mother. When a dart hit the rump of the darker cub, it squealed and twisted convulsively, trying to bite the metal tube, which was smaller than the one Terry had used on its mother. The honey-colored cub started to scurry away. Max was a good shot; his dart hit the cub in the shoulder. Its cry was pitiful.

In a matter of minutes, both cubs were sprawled on the ground next to their mother, unconscious.

"Better hurry," Max said.

"Don't worry, we got time," Terry answered. "Big mamma ain't gonna come to for a good while. We'll be outta here. Get the nets."

Miguel had been lying flat on his stomach, chin resting on his crossed arms. Now he scrunched forward, but he wasn't watching the men or the cubs; instead he was staring at the van. Jack could almost read Miguel's mind: The van meant only one thing to

Miguel—Seattle. He was scouting out the scene, trying to find a way to get into that delivery van without being caught. The fate of the bears was inconsequential to him, and although he'd been friendly enough to Jack and Ashley, both Landons were merely brief, interesting detours in his drive toward his goal.

Jack pulled Miguel's head close and whispered in his ear, "Don't do it. Those are bad men! If they see you, they'll see us, and we'll all get hurt. No!"

Miguel's large, dark eyes stared somberly into Jack's face. He didn't answer. Had Jack's words made any difference?

The two men pulled heavy netting from the back of the van. Dragging the drugged cubs by their back feet, they lifted them together onto the netting, wrapping them thoroughly like a bundle of loose watermelons, and then tying the netted package with ropes so that even when the cubs woke up, they'd be immobilized. After they were bundled securely, the men heaved them through the van's back doors.

"Got everything?" Terry asked. "Don't forget the chairs. And pick up those beer cans, just in case. We don't want to leave fingerprints."

The folding chairs went into the tailgate beside the sleeping cubs; the beer cans were thrown farther back, bouncing off the wall between the van's cargo area and the cab. Terry started the motor while Max hurried around to the passenger side, slamming his door.

The tires spun wildly. Jack's thoughts spun just as fast. Those guys had to be stopped, and he was the only one who could do it. Leaping to his feet, he pulled up Ashley and motioned to Miguel.

"Listen to me. They'll need to open the chain, so they'll have to park the van. Maybe we can rescue the cubs while the van is still behind the chain."

"But—they're grizzlies," Ashley protested.

"They're babies and they're zonked," Jack cried. "They can't hurt you. There's no time to argue—come on!"

Whether or not he understood, Miguel didn't need any urging. He ran ahead of Jack and Ashley, careful to stay out of sight of the two men in the delivery van, weaving through the trees in a footpath that led straight toward the chained entrance. For the van, it was a long drive around the loop from the spot where Max and Terry had set their trap, and because of the rough road, it moved slowly.

The three kids cut straight through the wild forest in the middle of the loop, shortening the distance, gaining time. When they came close to the campground entrance, still keeping hidden in the trees, Jack saw that the van had already arrived. From the inside, Max kicked open the passenger-side door, allowing heavy metal sound to pulse through the air as guitar riffs and drums shattered the stillness. Good, Jack thought. With that music, they won't be able to hear anything.

Timing would be crucial. There'd be no second chances.

Mentally, he tried to figure how long it would take the men to unlock the chain, hoping it would be long enough for him to carry out his plan. No time to think if it made sense. He had to try.

"Jack—we can't," Ashley panted. "You're crazy."

"I know." Gulping for air, he told them, "I'll open the back door and pull out the cubs. You help me, OK, Miguel?" He pointed to himself, then Miguel, then the van. Miguel nodded. "Ashley, stay here."

Jack took a deep breath and waited for Max to turn his back. "Start now!" he hissed, then darted from the underbrush. He prayed the men wouldn't see them, that Terry wouldn't look into the side-view mirror or Max turn around and catch them in the act. In seconds they were at the rear doors, protected by the van's bulky shape. With a quick jerk, Jack yanked on the handle of the right-hand door in the back of the van. He could feel Miguel pressed right behind him.

"What's the holdup?" Terry shouted through the driver's window.

"You got so dang many keys on this ring, I can't figure out which one is the master key."

"For cripe's sake," Terry complained, throwing open his door. "I showed it to you on the way in."

"I know, but there's a couple dozen keys here."

"You're nothing but an idiot!" Terry snapped. "That blasted music of yours has killed off all your brain cells."

A pause—Jack couldn't see, but he figured Terry was hurrying toward Max. Then Terry's voice snarled, "Give them to me!"

Jack felt another presence at his elbow, and for a second his stomach lurched, but when he turned, he saw his sister, pale, frightened, but resolute. A look passed between them, wordless but clear: She was there to help rescue the baby bears. Jack nodded and peered into the darkness.

There were no windows of any kind, just the metal hull with peeling paint on the floor. The two cubs, tied in netting, lay sound asleep, tangled together. Jack knew he'd have to move fast; they'd have, maybe, 20 seconds. He mentally counted the seconds as they worked—*20, 19....* Pulling on the netting, both boys slid the bundle of cubs through the partly open door, but it was too heavy. It dropped through their arms and landed hard. It was a good thing the baby bears were unconscious, or they would have squealed when they hit the dirt. No time to worry—*16, 15....*

"Now you got the right key, so open it, stupid," Terry yelled as he climbed back into the van. "Let's get outta here."

"I'm trying. And quit callin' me stupid."

"OK, brain dead."

14, 13.... "Ashley! Close the door," Jack whispered. *10, 9, 8....* Expertly, silently, Ashley pushed the back door until it latched. It took all the strength of all three kids to half-lift and half-drag the cubs toward the brush. Jack filled his mind with counting, ticking off the remaining seconds one by one—*7, 6, 5*.... If Terry looked into the van's mirror, he would see them. Don't think—*4, 3*.... The three of them dragged the cubs farther into the underbrush—*2, 1*.... As they staggered into the shelter of the nearest trees, where they paused to get a better grip, Ashley gasped, "They're heavy!"

Zero. Trying to keep their breathing low, they stopped where they were. Jack heard the van move forward, then heard Max get out once again to pull the chain across the entrance and lock it.

Suddenly Miguel jumped to his feet, murmuring, *"Hasta la vista,* dudes." Even as his index finger touched his forehead in a quick salute, he was leaping toward where the van still idled.

"Miguel's going!" Ashley cried.

Sometimes it's easier to ask forgiveness later than to get permission ahead of time, Jack had once heard. No time to think about it—they could hear Max's feet crunch in the gravel as the burly man neared the passenger side of the vehicle. As fast as a snake strike, Jack lunged forward and tackled Miguel around the ankles, dropping him to the ground. He pinned him flat, which wasn't hard since he outweighed Miguel by about 25 pounds. They heard Max open the passenger door, and then a sharp bang as it slammed shut.

Miguel let loose a stream of angry Spanish, but it

was too late—the moment was lost. The engine of the delivery van roared when it pulled away, bumping up the ungraded road, heading north, gravel sputtering from the tires in tiny showers.

When at last the sound of the van's engine faded, Miguel just stayed on the ground, lying facedown, no longer fighting. "Come on, get up," Jack said, lifting him. "It's OK, Miguel."

Tears welled up in Miguel's eyes and ran down his dusty cheeks. He stared at Jack and Ashley, mournfully. "Seattle," he said softly.

"I'm sorry—I—" Jack stammered.

"You can stay with us," Ashley told him.

Miguel didn't answer. Instead, he wiped his cheeks with his palms and turned away.

Maybe it *wouldn't* be easier to ask for forgiveness.

CHAPTER NINE

Soaring overhead, a hawk speared the sky with its beak before turning to plunge toward an open space beyond the trees. For a moment Jack watched its graceful force as it arced into the sky once more, another pivot, another bullet dive. The hawk knew what it was doing. It was working on instinct.

Standing there with Miguel, Ashley, and two grizzly cubs, Jack's thoughts blasted in every direction, like a string of firecrackers sputtering on the ground. Miguel, hurt and angry that he missed his ride; Ashley, fearful of the mamma grizzly; two drugged bear cubs tied in a net; a green delivery van that might be back any minute. Jack pictured the men and knew they were a threat, not only to those cubs, but to anyone who interfered with their plan to steal them. If only, Jack wished, he had the instinct of the hawk. If only he knew what to do now.

"Look, Jack, they're all squished together," Ashley said, trying in vain to pull the sleeping cubs apart. "The dark brown one is right on top of the honey one. Do you think the bottom cub will suffocate? Can you untie the knots?"

"I don't know. I'll try," Jack said. But undoing the knots in the ropes turned out to be impossible. They'd been pulled too tight even for Jack the Eagle Scout. His knuckles were scraped raw before he gave up. Sucking at the blood on one knuckle, he said, "That isn't working. And we can't just leave them here—if Terry and Max come back, they'll find them. We'll take them to our camp and cut open the net, then set them free. Miguel, grab an end. Ashley, you get across from me. Everyone pull up on the count of three. Ready?"

Ashley clutched the net, but Miguel didn't move. He kept his eyes to the ground. His shoulders, once squared, drooped like a candle left out in the sun. It was as if the life had gone out of him, a wick blown out.

"Come on, Miguel," Jack repeated. "Let's go!"

No response.

Immediately, Jack guessed what was wrong. Miguel had missed his ride. What did he care about two cubs, the very animals that cost him his chance? Not now, Jack moaned to himself. There was no time for this, no time for dealing with emotions when a clock was running. He had no idea how soon the tranquilizer would wear off. Thirty minutes? Ten? They had to do this fast. Planting himself right in front of Miguel, forcing Miguel's dark eyes to meet his, Jack spoke hurriedly. "Listen to me. I know you wanted to go." He thrust his hand out into the distance. "But those were bad men. Really bad. They would have hurt you. You couldn't go with them. I—I did what I had to do. So now you've got to help us with these cubs. I can't carry them with just Ashley alone."

Shaking his head softly, Miguel let his lids droop back toward the ground. All expression had drained from his face, like water into sand, and now there was nothing, just a blankness, a page with no writing. Maybe, Jack thought, this was how Miguel had survived. When things got rough, he just disappeared into himself.

"Miguel, I said I was sorry."

Silence.

"Come on, give me a break." Jack could hear his own voice rising. "Did you want to get yourself killed? We've got other problems now—like these bear cubs and…." Frustrated, Jack jerked his fingers though his hair. "I don't know how to explain! Why can't he understand—"

"Because you're yelling at him. He doesn't have to know English to hear that."

"OK," Jack snapped, "then you do it! Tell Miguel that if those guys found the cubs gone and just him in the back there, he would have been toast."

Ashley had been kneeling over the cubs, her fingers

kneading their backs through the netting. "Jack, it's not always what you say, but how you say it." She stood and gently, quietly, took Miguel's hand. "Miguel, I'm sorry you missed your ride. Jack is too. I know you've got to get to Seattle."

Miguel's eyes met hers. His gaze moved over her, warily.

"Seattle. *Sí,*" he answered, barely above a whisper.

"We—" she pointed to Jack, then to herself— "will try to get you there. To Seattle. To your teacher. I promise."

"Seattle?" A flicker of hope spread across Miguel's face. "*¿Es promesa?*"

"*Sí,*" Ashley answered. "A promise."

"Hey, you can't promise him that!" Jack exploded. "So that's your answer? To lie to him?"

"It's not a lie."

"How do you think you're going to—look, we don't have time for this. We've got major problems. We've got bear cubs all tangled up in this net, bad guys that may be headed back, a tranquilizer that's going to wear off—"

"And we've got Miguel. Maybe we could get him a bus ticket or something."

"Great. I thought you were going to adopt him," Jack retorted. "Now you're going to help him escape?"

"He's made it all this way. He deserves to get there." His sister's profile showed her chin sticking out stubbornly, which, Jack knew, meant she wasn't going to let go of her plan for Miguel.

Then Jack saw a smile tugging at the corner of Miguel's mouth as he said, *"Gracias."*

A squirrel chattered madly in a tree, doing its part to hurry them along. Precious time was ticking away.

"We're moving these cubs, now," Jack ordered, "with or without Miguel. Ashley, take this end." He pointed to the section he wanted his sister to lift. "Pull as hard as you can."

"Will you help us, Miguel?" Ashley asked.

"Help, yes," Miguel answered. Squatting low, he laced his brown fingers through the net. Ashley and Jack did the same. "OK," Jack barked. "On the count of three. Pull up!"

The heaviness of the two cubs—close to 150 pounds total, it felt like—was even more daunting because they were pure dead weight. Netting cut into the kids' fingers; they had to keep stopping to rub circulation back into their hands as they made their way up the straight part of the road, then turned left onto the loop that led to their campsite. Finally, about 30 feet from the trailer, they gave up and began to drag the sleeping cubs, who bounced along the ground like rocks in a bag. One of the cubs made a squeaking noise, but its eyes stayed closed.

"How long's it been since they were darted?" Ashley asked.

"I'm not sure, but we better get moving before they wake up."

"I'll get the scissors," Ashley volunteered. "It won't take long."

The scissors weren't any more of a success than the attempt to untie the knots. First Ashley, then Jack tried to squeeze the handles of the scissors together, but it was no use. "Darn it—there's wire in the center of this cord the net's made out of," Jack declared. "Mom's kitchen scissors aren't strong enough."

"Hey!" Miguel said, pointing to the darker cub, which was all tangled up with its honey-colored sibling. "She wake up."

Sure enough, the little bear's eyes were opening. Frightened, it began to yowl, at first in a little whimper, then louder in a hooting noise as it came more fully awake.

"I'm sorry, little baby," Ashley crooned. "We'll get you out real soon."

"We'd better. If it starts thrashing around, we're in big trouble. We need wire cutters." Jack tried to visualize the various things in the tailgate of the Jeep—cooler, battery cables, ponchos, two folded-up tarpaulins, a bucket, a roll of paper towels—but he couldn't remember seeing his dad's toolbox. "Ashley, go inside the trailer and check the compartment under the bench. If the toolbox is there, bring it."

The awakened baby bear was now howling up a

storm, protesting louder and louder, making so much racket its sibling had begun to stir.

"Jack—the other one's waking up, too. It's starting to move."

"Hurry, Ashley. Get me those wire cutters!"

Before she could move, they heard it. In the trees behind them, a rustling, snapping, then a shaking as if a storm were blowing through, except, Jack realized, there was no wind. The air was still and hot. The sound started up again, louder this time, as if a car were rolling toward them.

Miguel, eyes wide, stared in the direction of the noise and whispered, *"Dos hombres."*

"I see something," Ashley said shrilly. She seemed rooted to the ground, unable to move even when the crashing grew louder, as though an armored tank were breaking through the brush.

"There—where the branches are—ohmygosh! I think it's the.... It is! It's the *grizzly!"*

A shock like electricity jolted though Jack. Instantly, he was on his feet. "Into the Jeep!" he yelled. He grabbed Ashley's arm and yanked her hard. *"Go, go, go!* Miguel—the Jeep!"

"Run!" Ashley screamed. Her sneakers churned underneath her as she shot toward the Jeep. Praying that at least one of the doors was unlocked, Jack ran one step behind, commanding his legs to go faster, but his body felt trapped in a tangle of muscles and joints that wouldn't work together. The Jeep seemed a mile away. He heard the bear breaking through brush, and then she reached the clearing. Their camp.

Ashley ran full force into the Jeep: Her hands slapped the window to stop her headlong dash. She yanked on the back passenger door, but it wouldn't budge. In a split second she moved to the front, wrenching the handle and leaping inside in one continuous motion. Jack dove into the driver's seat and slammed the door hard behind him. Over the pounding of his heart he could hear the baby cubs cry in a cacophony of high-pitched cries and lower-pitched hoots. The mother grizzly roared her response. She barreled into the fire pit, teeth bared. Still drugged, staggering, she lurched out of the pit, her head wagging on her massive shoulders, guttural sounds exploding from her throat. She was less than ten feet away.

Ashley's hand gripped Jack's so hard he almost cried in pain. "Miguel! Where's Miguel?"

In the rearview mirror, Jack spotted him. Miguel was still beside the cubs, unmoving, frozen with fear.

Opening the door a crack, Jack screamed, "Miguel! You can make it! Come to the Jeep! Get in Ashley's side!"

Ashley's shriek was loud enough to penetrate her unopened window. *Miguel! She'll kill you! Come on!*

If he'd run toward Ashley's side, he would have made it. But, he ran in another direction, his feet kicking puffs of dirt as he raced toward the woods.

How many times had Jack been told that a human couldn't outrun a bear? "No human alive can run faster than a grizzly"—he'd heard it repeated since his first trip to Yellowstone, when he and Ashley were just toddlers. But Miguel didn't know that. Who would have told him? So Miguel raced, agile, wild, his arms pumping the air like pistons, his feet beating into the ground, his black hair flying.

Rising on her hind feet, her front paws dangling in front of her, the grizzly watched Miguel. Then, with an infuriated roar, she dropped on all fours and headed after him.

CHAPTER TEN

Though the grizzly was still too groggy to run as fast as she normally would, within seconds the gap between boy and bear narrowed to yards, then to feet.

"*No!*" Ashley screamed. "*Miguel!*"

It wouldn't help. Nothing could help. Miguel, Jack knew, was a dead man. There was nothing to be done. Miguel was about to be ripped apart, soft flesh to bone, and all Jack could do was watch as the bear overtook the boy. He heard a piercing scream from Miguel, whose eyes opened wide in terror as the bear caught up from behind.

"He's going to die!" Ashley cried hysterically.

Suddenly, the grizzly stopped her charge. Rearing once again on her haunches, she shook her head in confusion, as though not understanding what was happening to her. It's the drug, Jack thought. *Go, Miguel!*

Sensing he couldn't outrun the grizzly, Miguel took

the only escape route that might work: straight up! As nimble as a monkey, he grabbed a rough branch of a Douglas fir and heaved himself up to his hips, then swung his legs up and over the bough.

With her face pressed into the glass, Ashley yelled, "Yes! Hurry, Miguel! Go higher!"

Rocking and weaving, the bear swiped at Miguel, barely missing his leg. Miguel grabbed the next branch, but it broke off in his hands. When he reached for a higher branch, that broke, too. Wrapping his arms around the trunk, he wedged both feet against the rough bark, pressing hard with the soles of his ragged tennis shoes. Then, laboriously, moving only inches at a time, he began to shinny up the tree.

The female grizzly roared in fury. Raising herself to her full height, she lunged upward at Miguel, her claws missing him but leaving deep gouges in the bark of the trunk. *"¡Jesús, María!"* Miguel cried out. He struggled up to a safe branch just barely beyond the bear's reach; panting in fear, he clung there.

The grizzly circled the base of the tree, exhaling in great gusts of air like a bellows, growling, rearing up, ripping at the air before dropping back again to all fours. The drug in her system seemed to make her flounder between rage and confusion; she would stop, shake her head back and forth, then pace again. *Leave,* Jack prayed. *Just go.*

As quickly as she'd begun, she stopped pacing and

stood on her hind legs again, this time positioning her front paws against the tree trunk.

"She's climbing after him!" Ashley shrieked.

It was true. Hesitantly, then furiously, the grizzly sank her claws into the tree. She began to ascend, her back haunches thrusting as she pushed up through the bough spikes, snapping the smaller ones as if they were twigs. Screaming, "Help me!" Miguel shinnied even higher, but the top of the tree began to sway beneath his weight. There was nowhere left to go. The grizzly, though not adept at climbing, moved higher.

With her hind toes splayed against the trunk, she used her long claws to dig into the bark. Front paws cupped around the trunk, she climbed paw over paw, but at 350 pounds, her weight was too great for speed. Still, she climbed.

"She's going to get him! We've got to do something!" Ashley cried.

"Do what? We can't go out there—"

"We can't just sit here, either! Jack, he's going to die!"

"I know, I know, I *know!*" Jack pounded the wheel of the car. The car. He caught sight of the cup holder, where the keys lay. Without thinking it through enough to talk himself out of it, he grabbed the keys, inserted the Jeep key into the ignition, turned it hard and gunned the engine. The gearshift lever projected between the bucket seats like a letter *T.* Pressing his thumb into the button on the side of the gearshift, just as he'd seen his father do, he released the handle and slipped the arrow onto *R*.

"Jack—what are you doing?"

"Driving!"

"You don't know how—"

Whipping his head around so he could see behind him, Jack cried, "Put on your seat belt and shut up!"

The car lurched as he gave it some gas, moving faster than he thought possible in such a short distance. He was out of control, bumping over rocks and barely missing a stand of trees. When he slammed on the brakes, both he and Ashley whiplashed toward the dashboard before crashing back into their seats. Ahead of him, he saw the grizzly, her massive bulk struggling as she inched up the tree.

The shaft popped as Jack yanked the gearshift into Drive, then jerked the wheel to the right. Taking a breath, he slammed his foot on the gas pedal and immediately spun out of control. Too far! He'd bounced into the woods, snapping a small aspen tree at its base. Reversing again, he heard the tires sputter as he backed up onto the road.

"Jack!"

He jammed on the brake. Slower this time, he put his foot on the gas and eased the Jeep forward. His plan was simple—drive at the tree without hitting it in the hope that the motion of the car would scare the bear. A thousand things could go wrong, but he couldn't worry about that now; he had to focus on the one strategy he hoped would scare the bear away and save Miguel's life.

The steering wheel wanted to wrench from his hands; he gripped it, hard. Sweat moistened his palms. He was moving, heading for his target dead ahead. The grizzly was only 40 feet away from the Jeep, but it had climbed dangerously close to Miguel.

"What are you doing?" Ashley screamed. "If you hit the tree Miguel will fall out!"

"I'm not going to hit it."

She leaned into him hard and smacked the horn in a ferocious punch. "Scare her with the horn!" she cried. "Blast it!" The sound blared through the trees like a gunshot, and the bear, eight feet up now into the tree, reared back her head.

If he'd ever driven before in his life, his sister's sudden movement wouldn't have mattered. But Jack barely had control; Ashley's motion threw him off. In an instant he was bumping across the ruts on the road, and then, with a crash, he rammed up and over a log that had fallen on top of a boulder. The Jeep tilted at a crazy angle, its right front tire spinning helplessly in the air. The other three tires whined against the dirt, useless. Jack's shoulder jammed into the driver's door. Ashley flew into him, her head hitting his rib cage with a thud. Breath burst out of his chest, and for a split second Jack thought he would suffocate, until air sucked back into his lungs in a painful rush.

So this is what his plan had gotten him. The Jeep was wrecked, and Ashley—when he looked down, he saw she wasn't moving. Her head lay still, a round, dark circle against his chest. "Ashley," he gasped, "are you OK? Ashley!" He shook her harder than he meant to, and when he heard her snap at him he almost laughed with relief.

"Quit pushing at me. I'm fine." She righted herself, rubbing her elbow as she peered out the windshield. "How about you?"

"Fine. Sore. Where's the bear? Where's Miguel?"

"I don't know. I'm all turned around. Wait—over there. I see them! In the tree!"

Straining to sit up, Jack followed his sister's finger. It took a moment for his eyes to focus before he saw her—a large shape descending the tree, making its branches shake wildly as she moved down, slowly at first, then more rapidly.

"Look, Jack! It worked! You actually did it!"

"*We* did it," Jack answered softly.

All four legs moved paw under paw as the grizzly worked her way downward in reverse, slipping the last few feet like a fireman sliding down a pole. Her fur—paler across the hump and the shoulders, darker on the rump—rippled as she shook herself, finally standing on all fours at the base of the tree. Then she walked away from it, stumbling as she moved, her steps uneven, her front paws toeing in like parentheses.

"Oh, man, that was close. But Miguel—I think he's safe. As long as he stays up there." Ashley's breathing was rapid, shallow. One of her braids had come undone, coiling around her shoulder like smoke, and Jack could see white commas of fear around her nose and mouth. "OK, bear, you've scared us all half to death. Now go away."

But the bear's snout snuffed the air, as if searching for a scent. Wagging her head, she stopped directly in the path of the Jeep. Jack could see her eyes zero in on them, her stare as straight as a laser beam.

"She's looking our way. Jack, I don't like this."

"I don't like it either."

"Well, get us out of here."

"Ashley, I can't. We're stuck."

"But I don't like the way she's staring at us. Put it in reverse! Back us out!"

"The Jeep's stuck on a log. We've only got three wheels touching the ground. Listen, we're not going anywhere." Gunning the engine, Jack heard the tires grind into the dirt. He saw dirt clods spit into the road in a heavy shower. The noise and motion caught the attention of the grizzly. Her black nose moved as she sniffed the exhaust; she snorted.

"Stop it, Jack. The sound is making her mad!"

"I'm trying!"

The grizzly shook her head again and woofed,

sounding like a very loud big dog. Ashley's fingers clamped on Jack's forearm so tightly her nails dug into his skin like four tiny daggers. "Jack, Jack, Jack—she's coming toward us! It's like *Night of the Grizzlies*—she's—looking right at *me!*"

"It's OK," Jack assured his sister. "She's probably just heading for her babies. Listen, they're making an awful racket. She'll walk right past us and go for her babies, that's all. We're safe in here." He wished he knew that for sure. The Jeep ought to protect them, but what did he know? This grizzly'd been shot with some kind of drug that seemed to be causing volatile, unpredictable reactions. And she'd had her babies taken away. Jack knew that no animal on Earth was more dangerous than a mother bear protecting her cubs. In the background, hooting their fear in an unending series of *wooooohs* and howls, the cubs kept up their pathetic cries for their mamma. Everything was at its most explosive, like sparks dancing around a stack of dynamite. Anything could happen.

"I'm so scared," Ashley whispered.

"Just stay in the car," Jack told her as calmly as he could. "She can't hurt us."

"Don't let her get me."

"I won't."

"She's coming!" Ashley's voice rose in pitch. "Look at her, she's nearly—Lock the doors!"

All Jack's weight was against the driver's side.

Pulling forward, he pressed the small silver button to click down the locks. Jack never knew if it was that tiny sound or his movement, but something angered the grizzly. Instantly, she began to charge the Jeep, chewing up the distance like a train, her long claws scoring the ground as she ran straight toward them, mouth open, teeth bared.

Over his sister's scream, Jack barely heard his own voice as he whispered, "We're dead."

CHAPTER ELEVEN

The grizzly slammed into the Jeep with a force that jarred Jack's teeth. Staggering, the bear took two steps backward, her head swaying from side to side like a toy dog's. If Jack hadn't been so scared, he might have felt sorry for her. Whatever Terry had drugged her with was affecting her behavior. She seemed unable to focus. Confused, she backed up farther, stopped, and then charged again.

"Go away!" Ashley screamed, as the grizzly rammed the passenger side. The Jeep tipped lower on its left. Jack was smashed into the driver's window, his weight bearing down on his sore shoulder, his view a crazy jumble of the steering column and patches of sky. Ashley, trying to right herself, pushed off from Jack's headrest, her unbraided hair dangling like a rope ladder.

"We're going to tip over!" she cried.

"I—can't see—" Jack stammered.

"She's backing up. She's coming at us again—"

Wham! The grizzly's fury seemed to unleash itself against the Jeep. Roaring, she stood up to look into the passenger window. Now Jack could see, all right, and the vision made his heart freeze. Three hundred pounds of fury; a huge head with wide nostrils in a black nose pressed hard against the glass; two small, black-rimmed brown eyes staring; mouth open to reveal knifelike canine teeth that could tear through wood.

With a swipe of her claw, the grizzly savaged the hood of the Jeep, leaving deep, two-foot-long scratches. Illogically, Jack thought, I hope Dad won't blame that on me.

"The horn," Ashley whispered. "Blow the horn again. Scare her away."

The bear did flinch when the horn sounded, but instead of frightening her, it seemed to inflame her further. She began hitting the window on Ashley's side with both front paws, harder and harder.

"Ashley, climb into the backseat!" Jack yelled. If the bear shattered the front window, his sister would be dead meat.

For once, Ashley obeyed without arguing. Clambering over Jack, she jammed herself into the floor space between the front seat and the back, her spine pressed tightly against the far door, her arms twined around her legs. She'd made it just in time.

With one final thrust, the grizzly broke through the

front window, right where Ashley had been sitting. Because it was safety glass, the pane shattered into a cascade of diamond-shaped pebbles, spraying Jack and the whole interior of the Jeep. A few of the glass bits stuck to the bear's foot; while she huffed and sniffed and investigated her thick black paw, turning it up and nudging it with her nose, Jack pulled himself into a crouch. He grasped the rearview mirror with his left hand, balanced his right hand on the headrest behind him, and pressed his body into a curve against the car door: feet on the floor, stomach crowding the steering wheel, and head angled into the roof of the car.

With the window gone, Jack could clearly hear the sounds from outside: the hooting and yammering of the baby cubs, mostly, but there was something else—a louder hooting, sounding just like the cubs, but closer. Jerking his eyes to stare through the windshield, he saw—Miguel.

The boy had come down from the tree and now stood a dozen feet in front of the Jeep, making noises like the bear cubs, darting forward and then running back again, a few steps at a time. The big grizzly looked at Miguel, then at the Jeep, unsure which one deserved her attention. She picked the Jeep, and thrust her massive foreleg through the broken window to reach for Jack.

Too terrified to yell, Jack flattened himself against the door, sucking in his midriff as the bear's claws scraped across the steering wheel. He was barely out of reach. If she'd plunged the front part of her body—head, neck, and foreleg—through the opening, she'd have had him, but her leg alone wasn't long enough to cross the width of the Jeep.

Now Miguel was yelling, "Bear, bear, hey, *oso*. *¡Atención!*" and imitating those hooting sounds the cubs kept making, like the middle notes of a badly played clarinet. Miguel darted so close to the grizzly that if her foreleg hadn't been inside the Jeep, she could have clawed his face.

Looking from Jack to Miguel, the grizzly backed out of the Jeep. Immediately Miguel began to run, stopping every few yards to turn toward the bear and wave his arms, goading her on.

Ashley was on her feet now, clutching the seat back as she watched through the windows. "What's he doing?" she squealed, and Jack answered, "Saving our lives." Never in his life had he felt so scared or so helpless. And there was Miguel, risking his own neck to save Jack, who had betrayed him.

"Miguel, Miguel, Miguel." Ashley repeated it like a prayer as the boy ran away from the lumbering grizzly. "He's heading toward the pump!"

"Yes! The pump!" Jack raised his right fist in excitement because right away he could picture what Miguel was planning.

Miguel reached the pump just seconds before the

bear did. He pulled up the sheet metal cover on the compartment housing the pipes, dived inside, and pulled the lid down on top of him.

Ashley collapsed against Jack, sobbing, "He made it."

Not wanting to frighten her, Jack didn't answer. Miguel was safe, but only for the moment. How long would it take before the bear managed to lift the lid with her long, lethal claws? Bears were smart and could use those claws almost like fingers. For now the grizzly just prowled around the lid, snuffling, growling, head down, the massive muscles of her shoulders hunched.

And then came the rumble of a truck's engine. Doors opened. Jack's heart sank. Were the poachers coming back?

If they were, they could grab the cubs, still tied up in the netting, and get away with them before the mother grizzly figured out that she should go after the real bad guys and forget about Jack and Ashley and Miguel, who'd only been trying to help. At first Jack couldn't see what was happening because of the trees, but then he heard a sound he could no way have expected: barking.

It all happened so fast! Before he knew it, his mother was running toward him. Beyond her were three women. Each woman held a black-and-white dog on a leash, and each dog was barking furiously at the female grizzly. The woman in the lead fired a shotgun at the bear as she shouted, "Go away, bear! Get out of here, bear! Get out of here!"

Olivia, looking frantic, had reached the Jeep and wrenched at the door, reaching through the broken window to release the lock. In an instant she pulled out her children, crying, "Are you all right? Are you hurt?"

"We're fine," Ashley cried, "but Mom, that woman is shooting the bear!"

"That's Carrie Hunt and she knows what she's doing. She's firing rubber bullets and firecracker shell rounds. They won't hurt the bear."

The grizzly, forgetting Miguel, stood up to face the three dogs and their unceasing barrage of barks. The loud noise of exploding firecrackers blasted Jack's ears as he yelled, "Mom, we gotta get her cubs. They're tied up back there. Where are Dad's wire cutters?"

"You've got her cubs? No wonder she's—" Olivia pointed to the tailgate. "The cutters—they're inside the box with the starter cables."

Ashley wailed, "I don't want Jack to go out there, Mom. It's too dangerous!"

"I'll be with him. You stay here. The bear doesn't want to hurt any of us—she just wants her cubs." When Ashley still looked frightened, Olivia added, "See the other two women with Carrie? One's a handler named Angela, and there's Ali, the ranger, with the third dog. All three of them will stay between us and the bear, and the dogs will keep barking. Look—they're already getting the bear to move back into the trees."

Loping, the grizzly had turned toward the thickest stand of Douglas fir. As she ran into the shelter of the woods she made all kinds of worried sounds—barks, grunts, roars, all of them combining with the steadily accelerating barking of the dogs, the shouts of the women dog handlers, and the explosion of fire-cracker shells.

Cutters in hand, Jack raced down the path to reach the cubs. He cut through the cord-wrapped wires of the net that held them while his mother pulled the cubs free of the netting and gently set them onto their feet. Freed at last, they stood up, gingerly trying out their legs, terrified by the presence of so many people plus the wildly barking dogs, not knowing whether they should risk a dash to reach their mother.

Hearing her babies squealing and bawling, the agitated female grizzly came out of the trees once again and started toward them, but Carrie let loose another barrage of rubber bullets. Bending forward toward her lead dog, she spoke to it just loudly enough for Jack to hear, saying, "Cassie, this is going to be a hard one. She thinks we're going to hurt her babies. We need to let her know that if she stays back, we won't hurt her or the cubs either."

Cassie, the lead dog, doubled her barking, while Angela and Ali encouraged their dogs to do the same, shouting, "Bark at the bear! Bark at the bear!"

When the mother grizzly once again retreated into the trees, Carrie instructed, "OK. Ali, Angela, pull the dogs back now so the cubs can go to their mother. Olivia, have your children back up behind us. We need to stay together so we don't look like a threat. Let's clear a path and keep real quiet."

The cubs, stumbling, took a few hesitant steps in the direction of their mother and then took off, their back legs tucked under them as they scooted toward her. When they got close, the female grizzly rushed to them, sniffing each one thoroughly to discover whether they'd been harmed. Maybe it was knowing that the cubs were safe, but the rage seemed to seep out of her. She was wary but no longer interested in Jack or Ashley or anyone else. Woofing, she hurried her cubs into the trees. One behind the other, they followed their mother until all three bears were hidden by the foliage.

"They're gone! Thank heavens!" With the bears out of sight, Olivia took a deep breath and said in a trembling voice, *"Now* can someone please tell me what's been going on here? I mean everything! Starting from the beginning."

Ashley was about to answer, but Jack shook his head and said, "Wait." Taking his mother's hand, he said, "Explanations later. Come on, Ashley. There's something we have to show Mom." With Ashley on one side of Olivia and Jack on the other, they led their mother toward the pump.

"All clear!" Jack yelled as they approached it. *"Es bueno,* dude! You can come out."

By only an inch, the sheet metal lid moved upward. After a wait that seemed minutes long but probably was just a few seconds, the lid rose another inch. Then, slowly, like the top of a coffin in an old vampire movie, the metal lid squeaked open a little at a time, until it was high enough to reveal Miguel jammed inside the concrete compartment, his slight body twisted between the pipes. With a final thrust, Miguel flipped the lid all the way open until it banged on the ground on the other side.

Laughing, Jack grabbed Miguel's hand and pulled him to his feet. Ashley was laughing, too—at the astonishment on Olivia's face. "Mom," she said, "this is Miguel. He's from Mexico. Say hello to our mother, Miguel."

"Buenos días, Señora," Miguel said, and gave a little bow.

Fifteen minutes later, after the most basic explanations had been made, Olivia kept hugging Jack and Ashley, saying, "I never should have left you two alone here." And then she'd hug them again and look them in the eyes and ask, "Are you sure you're alright?"

"We're OK, Mom," Jack kept telling her, but Ashley just nestled into Olivia's hugs.

Carrie, the leader of the bear dog team, said to the kids, "Your mother asked me to drive her back here so she could show you the dogs, but I never expected you were going to get a demonstration."

"That bear—" Ashley began. "Mom, I was so scared!"

"I'm sure you were, poor baby," Olivia answered, hugging Ashley again.

Angela told them, "The way the grizzly was acting makes me think those men used an old, outdated drug when they darted her. Years back, bears got darted with something called Sernylan."

"Yeah, you might have heard of it," Ali added. "When it's sold by street dealers, it's called angel dust. It put the bears to sleep fast, all right, but the park people quit using it because it's no longer manufactured legally."

Carrie, kneeling next to the panting dogs as she rubbed their necks affectionately, looked up to explain, "Some bears, when they started to come out of that drug Sernylan, would fixate on movement and charge at anything that was moving anywhere near them. I imagine that's what was going on with this grizzly." She tilted her head back as the dogs licked her chin, then added, "And even in her drugged state, that poor mamma bear kept hearing her cubs bawling. No wonder she reacted the way she did, charging you kids."

Ashley shuddered in Olivia's arms before she said, "But Mom, everything that happened—that wasn't the bear's fault. Terry and Max lured her with a dead deer for bait, and then they shot her with drugs. So she shouldn't be destroyed. That would be so wrong."

"Don't worry, she won't be destroyed," Carrie assured Ashley. "When a mother's defending her cubs, the park doesn't punish her. In fact, that grizzly was very good to us. Even though she was afraid for her babies, she stood back when we confronted her. Most bears really don't want trouble, and they'll do the right thing if you just give them the chance."

As Carrie moved away, Miguel took her place, sitting on the ground to pet the dogs, who seemed to tolerate the petting rather than encourage it. So many words were flying around while Jack and Ashley and the women discussed what had happened, Miguel must have given up trying to understand. When Carrie and the handlers gave each dog a treat of beef jerky and told them, "Good job on the bear," Miguel shyly held out his hand. For a minute Jack thought Miguel was asking for some jerky so he could eat it himself, but when Carrie handed him a piece, he fed it to the lead dog, Cassie, who licked Miguel's salty fingers.

On the long drive to Glacier, Olivia had talked a lot about the Wind River Bear Institute. Carrie Hunt—small, blond, wiry and energetic—had devised a whole new way to handle problem bears. With pepper spray, rubber bullets, and the constant, continuous barking of her specially trained Karelian bear dogs, she aimed to teach bears to stay away from humans and from occupied places, like cabins. Sometimes a few encounters between a bear and the dogs was all it took. If the bear got the message—*Do not approach people or their things*—its life could be saved.

"After the mamma bear left with her babies," Ali said now, "I phoned park headquarters. They told me they'd radio every law-enforcement ranger in a 20-mile radius of Quartz Creek and send them here. The rangers ought to begin arriving soon. Oh, they said to tell you kids that you gave a good description of that van. Good work, guys."

Jack growled, "I hope the rangers get here before the poachers do. I'd just love to watch those guys get busted."

"*If* the poachers come back at all," Olivia added. "What I'd like to find out is what they intended to do with the cubs. And if they've taken other cubs before this. If they have, that might solve the mystery of all those missing second-year cubs."

Sounding startlingly out of place in that wooded setting, Ali's cell phone rang. She flipped it open and switched it on, then listened for a long while before she said, "Wow! OK. I'll tell them." Closing the phone, she announced, "The state police think they've spotted the van. They didn't stop it because it looks like it's on its way back to Quartz Creek. Approximate time of arrival is 20 minutes!"

"That's a 'wow' all right," Jack agreed.

"There's more. Several law-enforcement rangers are near us now, but they're going to park their vehicles a distance away so the poachers won't see them. Carrie, you're supposed to move your truck a ways down the road, and you and Angela stay inside it with the dogs to keep them quiet."

Just then two of the law-enforcement rangers arrived, their guns strapped to their belts. After a few quick words, they instructed, "As soon as we get word the van's getting close, I want all of you people to disappear. It's possible these men are armed. We don't know what we're in for. The rangers will take cover in the trees. Ma'am," he said to Olivia, "is that your camping trailer back there at that site way down the loop?"

When Olivia nodded, he said, "I guess it's far enough away, and it's hidden behind the trees, so it ought to be safe. I want you to go there right now, and I want you and those kids to stay inside.

"We don't want those poachers grabbing one of you to create a hostage situation," the second ranger added.

Frowning, the first ranger complained, "Hey, Roger, you didn't need to tell them that part."

"Thought they ought to know. It'll make them more careful," Roger answered, checking his gun to see that it was ready.

A chill went through Jack. Hadn't they had enough scary stuff for one day? Now it looked like they'd be witness to an ambush! Miguel must be clueless about what was going to happen; Jack ought to try to explain.

But Miguel was nowhere to be seen. Neither was Ashley.

He found both of them huddled on the dirt under the camper trailer. "He thinks they're immigration officers, and they've come to get him," Ashley whispered to Jack when she saw his bent head appear at ground level. "I'm trying to tell him that they're just rangers, and they won't arrest him."

"It's OK," Jack assured Miguel. "Remember the promise? Seattle. Promise." Jack made an *X* on his chest with his finger. Did kids in Mexico use the same sign for "cross my heart"?

Staring first at Ashley, then at Jack with those big, dark eyes, Miguel nodded and crawled out from underneath the trailer.

CHAPTER TWELVE

Tension mounted as more rangers arrived on foot, listening to dispatches on two-way radios, conferring among themselves. Standing just outside the Landons' camping trailer, Jack watched the rangers, impressed that they acted so professionally—not scared or nervous, like he was. Finally one of them said, "Just got the word that the delivery van is less than two miles away. On this road that means about 15 more minutes. Everyone take cover, and don't come out until I tell you it's safe."

"Get inside the trailer," Olivia said to the kids. "On the floor. Now!"

"But I want to see what's going on! Can I use the binoculars and watch from behind the door?" Jack asked. "The door's metal, too. I'll watch just until they drive up, OK, Mom?"

"Except we don't know where the binoculars are,"

Ashley quickly added. "Do you know where Dad left them, Mom?"

"In the drawer under our bed. But I don't know if this is a good idea. It's not safe."

"From way back here? We can hardly even see the Quartz Creek entrance through all those trees. Come on, Mom," Ashley begged, "I want to see what the rangers are doing, too! *Please?*"

Their mother hesitated. "Maybe we can lower the top part of the door, but only by an inch or two. If you see that van, then I want you down on that floor flat. Understood?"

Jack nodded. Grabbing Miguel's arm, he steered him inside the trailer, where the air was hot, the walls were made of easily penetrated canvas, and the slightly opened top section of the door provided only the narrowest view of the campground. After scrounging around in a drawer, Olivia pressed a pair of binoculars into Jack's hand. "Be careful," she said. "And this is only till the van comes."

"Hey, what about me?" Ashley complained.

"We'll share," Jack told her quickly. "Just give me a second, Ashley. Then we'll trade."

The binoculars pressed into his eye sockets as he peered through the two-inch space above the sliding part of the metal door. At first he couldn't detect a single Smokey Bear uniform, because they blended perfectly with the underbrush, but when he moved his head a little he spotted a ranger in the distance with his back against a tree. "OK," Jack muttered to himself, "I found you guys. Now, where's the entrance?"

The loop their camper was parked on meandered south before joining the straight part of the lane, which jutted west. If he looked diagonally through the trees, Jack could barely make out a post and a bit of chain at the entrance.

"My turn, Jack," Ashley declared, crowding next to him.

Sighing, Jack passed the binoculars. Moments later, Ashley passed them back. As the minutes crawled by, they switched places and possession, as if the binoculars were a pendulum. Miguel sat quietly next to Olivia, who was perched on her bed, nervously tapping her foot, waiting. It seemed to take forever before they heard the engine and then the sound of tires spitting stones on the rough road. Jack was lucky enough to have the binoculars in his hands when the van approached. "They're here," he said quietly.

"Down. Now. Everyone," Olivia ordered. As Ashley, Miguel, and Olivia dropped to the trailer floor, Jack strained for one last look. The rangers were so motionless he could barely see them. Terry and Max would never suspect an ambush.

"Heads up, rangers," Jack whispered.

"Jack, get down," his mother ordered.

"Just one more second!"

The engine idled as one door slammed. Max must be getting out to unlock the chain. "Don't lock it up again," Terry yelled. "I don't want to mess with it on the way out."

The tires made a thudding sound as they rolled across the lowered chain. Slowly the van drove into Jack's view. When it stopped, both men got out to look around.

"I still think it was you," Terry snarled loudly. "I have an idiot for a partner."

"They don't have a gun," Jack whispered. "They're arguing. One of the rangers just moved closer."

"I swear," Max said, "those cubs were inside, sleeping, when I shut the back door. Maybe they fell out when we stopped to open the gate here." Even across the distance, his voice was loud enough to be heard. "Maybe they wiggled around until they got in the underbrush. Maybe—"

Terry answered, "You say 'maybe' one more time, I swear I'll knock you flat. Just look around. If they're not here, we'll go back to where we loaded them. Whatever happened, they oughta still be in the net, so we'll find them." Terry and Max began prodding the underbrush, pulling back branches, peering into the thick stands of trees.

"Jack Landon, you get down on this floor or you're going to be in serious trouble," Olivia hissed. Jack had just lowered the binoculars when, out of nowhere, he heard a faint sound that grew steadily louder. *Whistling!* Someone was whistling!

"Wait, Mom." Jack raised the binoculars again and looked out. He could tell Max and Terry heard the whistling, too. They stood stock still, searching for the source.

Jack gasped, "Oh no! Not now!"

Trudging along the path made by the tire tracks was Steven Landon, his lips pursed as he trilled a tune. When he spotted Terry and Max, he slowed down.

"Mom, it's Dad," Jack whispered frantically. "He's out there. What'll we do?"

Olivia scrambled to her feet and snatched the binoculars from Jack's hand. She didn't seem to notice that Jack was still at her side. He could see well enough to make out his father's surprised expression.

"Hi there," Steven called out to the two poachers. "I'm sorry to have to tell you this, but Quartz Creek is a closed campground. Is there anything I can help you with?"

Terry looked Steven up and down, from his floppy-brimmed hat and politely smiling face, past the backpack bristling with tripod and monopod and bulging with camera equipment, to his long, thin, muscular legs and the thick socks and mountain boots. Terry must have been trying to figure out whether Steven was a park employee or just a hiker.

"Yeah," Terry answered. "We know how this campground's shut down." He stepped forward, his arms closing over his chest so that muscles bulged through his T-shirt. "It's OK—we're with the park."

When Steven's brow wrinkled in doubt, Terry jerked his thumb at Max. "Me and my friend Paul, we're off duty. That's why we're out of uniform."

"Oh." Steven nodded a bit uncertainly, eyeing Terry's Greek fisherman's hat and mirrored sunglasses. "So you were able to get in here—"

"With our key," Max finished, holding it up. "Park people always have keys." Terry shot him a look, and Max quickly dropped the key ring into his pocket.

"Like you just said, this campground is closed. So what are you doing in here?" Terry asked.

"We—my wife, Olivia, and I—are here because of the bear cubs. You know, the ones that are missing? If you're with the Park Service, you're probably familiar with—"

"Bear cubs?" Terry asked, heat rising in his voice as he moved closer to Steven. "Grizzly bear cubs? You know about that?"

"Absolutely," Steven answered. "Is that why you're here, too?"

Next to Jack, Olivia groaned softly, "Please, Steven, just get out of there!"

"We're here 'cause of the cubs. Yeah," Max nodded. "You got it, man."

"Wait—are we talking about the same thing?" Terry

interrupted. "Grizzly cubs. About yay big?" He lowered his hand to his kneecap to show the height of a second-year cub. "You're telling me you know what happened to them?"

Pushing back his hat, Steven rubbed his forehead. "Well, not exactly. Olivia—Dr. Landon—knows more about it than I do."

"Oh, she does, does she?"

Inside the trailer, Jack said softly, "Mom, they think Dad's talking about the cubs they put in the net. They think Dad's got them!"

Olivia didn't answer. She kept her eyes on Steven, while her fingers clenched tightly around the binoculars.

"...so you'd just better tell Olivia that I want them back," Terry threatened.

"Want them back? Well, sure, all of us want to get them back," Steven said, slowly moving away.

"Where do you think you're going?" Terry snarled. "I said I want those cubs. Right now!"

Jack's pulse began to pound as Terry slipped his right hand beneath his shirt and pulled out a—

"He's got a gun!" Olivia's voice caught in her throat. "Oh no, don't let him—"

Terry took another step toward Steven, who moved backward, his hands spreading into the air as he asked, "Whoa—what do you need a gun for?"

"To blow your head off if you don't bring back those cubs."

"What—what cubs?"

"Don't mess with me, man! Get that Olivia chick to give them to me, or I swear—"

Suddenly an amplified electronic voice blasted out of the trees. "PUT THE GUN DOWN." Terry whirled, no doubt recognizing a police bullhorn when he heard one.

Hostage situation! The words hit Jack's brain like a cymbal crash. If Terry or Max grabbed Steven to use as a shield, all those law-enforcement rangers standing in the trees with their guns drawn would be just so much useless firepower.

As loud as he could, Jack yelled, *"Run, Dad!"* Olivia grabbed Jack, screaming, *"No!"* but Steven took off running just a second before Max lunged for him—Max's hands missed him by inches. At the same instant, half a dozen rangers leaped out from the woods to form a circle around Terry and Max.

Dumbfounded, the poachers saw six military-style handguns held straight out and steady, with the muzzles of the gun barrels staring at them like unblinking eyes. It was as though all motion died. Halfway to the trailer, Steven froze. Even the birds stopped chirping in the trees.

"Don't shoot!" Terry yelled, throwing his own gun to the ground.

As the rangers moved forward to handcuff both men, Olivia dashed out of the trailer, running so fast she pushed through underbrush as if it were cotton candy. When she reached Steven, she threw her arms around him so tightly it seemed as though they were one person instead of two.

Jack and Ashley followed close behind. "Yay, Dad!" Ashley cried, catapulting herself into the hug. Jack hung back, unsure, until his mother reached out and pulled him in. The four of them crushed together. Now that they were safe, Jack suddenly felt his throat tighten with so much emotion he almost couldn't breathe. They'd made it. All of them.

It was over.

"Twenty-four hours," Steven said, shaking his head. "How could so much have happened in just twenty-four hours? Last night at this time we were sitting around the campfire listening to Jack tell a story about a buffalo runner and his little sister."

"And before that," Ashley said, "we were at Ulm Pishkun, where we heard the true story of the buffalo runners. But I have to say something," she told them, rising from the picnic bench where the whole family was seated. "No buffalo runner could ever have been braver than Miguel was today. To save Jack and me, he got the grizzly to chase after him, because he knew in one more minute we were going to get mauled."

Jack stood, too, and raised his can of cola in a salute.

"Here's to Miguel," he said, and everyone cheered, while Miguel beamed.

"To Miguel...Montoya!" Olivia repeated.

Miguel's dark eyes opened wide. He whispered in Ashley's ear.

"He wants to know how you found out his last name," she reported.

"He was in the newspaper, remember?" Olivia said, smiling. "Miguel Montoya, the runaway from Nogales, Mexico. That is you, isn't it?"

Miguel must have understood "newspaper." He looked half proud and half scared. "Is true?" he asked. "In newspaper?"

Jack was getting an idea. It took root and grew while he examined it in all directions, liking the feel of it. "Mom and Dad," he said, "if Miguel's story was interesting enough to make it into the newspaper a couple of days ago—I mean, just the story about him crossing the border on his own—what would happen if we told reporters what he did today? About how he saved our lives?"

Steven cocked an eyebrow, considering. "Sure, we could do that, but what purpose would it serve?"

Ashley cried, "I get it! If we told everyone Miguel's a hero, they wouldn't send him back to Mexico. Mom, we promised we'd get him to Seattle."

Olivia frowned when she heard that. Mildly admonishing Ashley—Olivia couldn't bring herself to scold her children, not tonight, not after the near miss with the grizzly—she said, "You had no business promising. His case is a problem for the Immigration Service. He's an illegal alien, Ashley."

Miguel recognized those words, all right. He cowered, shrinking beneath the edge of the picnic table as though he wanted to disappear.

"He's a hero!" Ashley declared vehemently. "He saved us."

"Take it easy," Steven told her. "I think it's possible we could arrange to have Miguel stay in this country. We could be his sponsors."

Slapping the table, Jack said, "He doesn't want us. He wants to go to his teacher in Seattle. If she found out what he's gone through, I know she'd sponsor him herself."

Everyone was silent. The fire crackled in the fire pit while Steven and Olivia pondered Miguel's situation. "Ms. Lopez," Olivia suddenly announced.

"Huh?"

"Ms. Lopez, the head of Social Services in Jackson Hole, the one who arranges all the emergency-care foster placements for the kids that come to our family. She might have connections with Immigration and Naturalization. And she speaks Spanish."

"Call her," Ashley demanded. "You have our cell phone, don't you? Will it work out here?"

"I think so. I'll give it a try."

"Hey, guys," Steven protested. "Shouldn't we be roasting marshmallows or something? We're supposed to be having a wilderness experience out here under the stars, and you want to bring in all this modern technology." When he saw the expressions on all their faces, he shrugged and said, "OK, I give up. Make the call, Olivia."

In her job, Ms. Lopez was used to phone calls at unusual hours, both day and night. After Olivia briefly explained the situation, she handed the phone to Miguel. "Here. Talk to her," she told him.

Miguel clapped a hand over his mouth as his eyes grew wide with apprehension. Olivia said gently, "There's nothing to be afraid of. This nice lady wants to talk to you, Miguel."

But Miguel refused to take the phone. "Hold on," Olivia said to Ms. Lopez. Then, "Miguel, do you know what this is?" She held up the cell phone.

He nodded. *"Teléfono."*

"That's right. Have you ever talked on one?"

Miguel shook his head. My gosh, Jack thought, he's never made a phone call. How many kids like Miguel don't even know how to use a phone? Where he lives there's no electricity and no running water, so why would there be a telephone? He's clueless, and scared.

"See this? You listen with this part," Jack instructed, holding the earpiece to his own ear. "Then you talk in this part, like my mother was doing."

"Go ahead, Ms. Lopez," Olivia called out. "Miguel is ready."

Lifting the cell phone in a shaking hand, as if it might be a grenade ready to explode against his ear, Miguel sat rigid, staring dead ahead. Then he straightened, and a grin crept over his lips. *"Sí,"* he kept saying, until finally he let loose a barrage of Spanish that went on and on until, reluctantly, he handed the phone back to Olivia.

After the call was over, Olivia told everyone, "She's going to do everything she can. Since we're certified foster parents, she'll fix it so that we can keep Miguel for the next couple of days while she goes through all the red tape with Immigration."

"Yay!" Jack and Ashley both yelled, and Ashley hugged Miguel, who didn't seem to mind the hug.

"Marshmallows, anyone?" Steven asked, but just then the cell phone rang. "Oh, good grief! Can't get away from it," he moaned, grabbing the phone to flick it open.

He listened. And listened, speaking only a few words like, "What? Yes. Definitely. At headquarters tomorrow? We'll be there. Oh yeah, I have to get my Jeep fixed. Window smashed out. You'll let us use a park vehicle? Great!"

"Well," he said, leaning back as he shoved down the antenna and closed the phone. "Have I got news for all of you!"

"What, Dad?" they asked. "Tell us."

"Mmmmmm," Steven teased, "maybe I'll save it till after the marshmallows."

"Dad!" Ashley and Jack ran around the table to wrestle with their father, Ashley messing his hair while Jack knuckled him in the ribs, shouting, "Come on—tell us!"

"OK," Steven said. "I shouldn't be goofing around. This is not a happy story."

That got them silent in a hurry. "Why?" Jack asked, but Steven had already turned to Olivia, saying, "I think we've solved the mystery of the vanishing cubs."

He went on to tell them that the delivery van had been traced to a game ranch on an island off the coast of Seattle, where hunters paid tens of thousands of dollars to shoot exotic animals. "Not just grizzlies," Steven said, "but mountain lions, wolves, bison, wild boars—animals that are protected or endangered." It had been happening for several years, he said: Young animals were stolen or bought illegally, then taken to the island ranch, where they got fed regularly so that they never learned to fend for themselves in the wild. Almost tame, they'd be turned out when they became adults to become the quarry of rich, inexperienced hunters who could track them down without much effort, then shoot them for big-game trophies to hang on a wall.

"That's awful!" Jack exclaimed.

"For sure! But thanks to you," Steven said, "the owners will be arrested. I hope they get jail time. First thing tomorrow, we have to go to park headquarters, because Kate Kendall, the woman in charge of the bear DNA project, wants you kids to tell her everything you saw happening to the bears today. She's leaving tomorrow for Seattle to go to the game ranch. With her DNA samples, she might be able to tell how many of the bears there came from Glacier."

"They'll be returned here, won't they?" Jack asked.

Olivia paused before she answered slowly, "It's going to be a problem. If the bears were fed regularly by the people at that ranch, they won't be able to adjust to the wild."

Ashley drew in her breath. "A fed bear is a dead bear. Oh Mom—Couldn't they go to zoos?"

"Maybe. Some of them." Steven nodded, but Jack saw the look in his father's eyes. He was just trying to comfort Ashley.

"It's heartbreaking," Olivia agreed. "But you three kids ought to feel really good. Today you saved two little grizzly cubs from going to that awful hunting ranch. You saved their lives."

"And Miguel saved ours," Ashley said.

CHAPTER THIRTEEN

Color seemed to radiate from Going-to-the-Sun Road, and as the five of them wound toward the summit, Jack felt as though he couldn't take in the beauty fast enough. Wildflowers splashed the slopes in a shower of jewels, pink clusters called shooting stars, then fireweed that blazed like candles next to blossoms the color of topaz, all scattered against a carpet of velvety green. There were 1,200 species of flowering plants in Glacier, Jack had been told, and he believed it. It was as if a giant box of crayons had been spilled out, one against another in endless patterns of browns and emeralds, purples and scarlets—every color under the sun.

"Dad, stop for a picture, OK?" Jack pleaded.

"We pulled over five minutes ago and five minutes before that. Sorry, I've got to keep driving. Otherwise, we won't reach the lake until autumn."

"But Dad, it's the perfect shot. Look, it couldn't be

any better. Come on, I've got to get this one."

"There'll be another perfect shot around the next bend. I'm afraid you'll have to let this one go by. Just try to keep it in your mind's eye."

Above, soaring rock faces towered over their car like enormous giants; below, shimmering windswept waters winked in the morning light. There was so much to see that Jack was almost frustrated as he attempted to absorb it all, to remember it.

Miguel, too, watched wide-eyed, his face pressed flat into the glass while Jack gazed out of the driver's side. Ashley, jammed between them, could still see enough to say, "Wow."

"Es bonita," Miguel said softly.

"Sí," Ashley agreed. *"Muy bonita."*

Miguel seemed to be enjoying the three days he'd spent with the Landons as they toured as much of Glacier as they could squeeze in. Their Jeep was being repaired in the nearby town of Hungry Horse, so the park had loaned them an Explorer to travel around in. The delay was fine with Jack; it gave them a chance to be explorers. They'd traveled down the Trail of the Cedars boardwalk, amazed at the tropical feel of it: Pillars of shaggy barked cedars stood next to black cottonwood surrounded by green ferns and mosses. They'd seen waterfalls slicing glaciated peaks, and water so clear it seemed the fish swimming in it were flying in air. They'd seen mountain slopes thick with huckleberries. They'd watched in wonder as a moose forded a stream, its long legs strangely delicate, like a dancer prancing across a stage.

Still, all the Landons felt tension as they waited to see what would become of Miguel; the worry never quite left any of them. The only one who didn't seem concerned about his fate was Miguel himself. Content to enjoy each day, he drank in the images of Glacier, breaking into a wide smile whenever he spotted a wild animal.

If Jack hadn't questioned his mother earlier, he'd have thought everything was fine. But when Olivia reported her conversation with Ms. Lopez, Jack's heart sank.

"She said Miguel can stay with us until Social Services figures out the next step, but he very well might have to go back to Mexico. She told me when she tried to explain it to Miguel in Spanish, he didn't seem to understand. He kept telling her he had to reach Seattle. She asked us to keep a close eye on him, in case he tries to run away."

But he didn't try to run, not once. Whatever Miguel expected his fate to be, for the present he seemed happy. Ashley thought it was because Miguel had never seen anything like the spectacular beauty of Glacier, but Jack guessed it was more. With the Landons, Miguel was fed. He had warm clothes and a bed. He belonged. He no longer faced the world alone.

Jack knew, though, that one phone call from Ms. Lopez could change everything. Square-jawed men from the Department of Immigration and Naturalization— well, maybe they wouldn't have square jaws, but that was the way Jack pictured them—could appear and take Miguel away, back to his life of poverty. How could he return to that harsh existence when now he knew how many good things were in the world? All Miguel wanted was to change his life, and the lives of his family in Mexico. He was braver than anyone Jack had ever met. He'd saved their lives. Would it cost the United States so much to give him a chance?

In the car, Jack felt Miguel's elbow in his ribs as the boy eagerly pointed to the side of the road. Up ahead, white animals scampered across a mountain slope like bits of clouds. Miguel's face lit up as he chattered a string of Spanish words before he stopped to slowly translate.

"Look—over there. See…uh…." He shook his head, unable to come up with the English word.

"Yeah, I see them!" Jack exclaimed. "Mountain goats! There's a whole bunch of them—they look like they're hanging straight up on the side of that mountain. How do they do that? Dad, *now* will you pull over so I can get a picture?" he begged.

"You bet. I'll grab my camera, too."

The car had barely pulled into a parking spot when the cell phone rang, loud and penetrating. Every one of them froze. Only one person would be calling them: Ms. Lopez. The phone shrilled again. Olivia hesitated just a moment before answering it. "Hello?" she said. "Oh, hello. Yes, I can hear you fine, Ms. Lopez."

Jack felt his stomach clench. For the first time since they'd begun their tour of Glacier, Miguel's face clouded. He looked from Olivia, to Steven, to Jack, and then to Ashley.

"Yes, we're all fine. Miguel's been a delight. And he's got quite the appetite—I've never seen anyone that small eat so much. No, no, don't worry about the bill. It was fun just to watch him enjoy himself."

Jack saw Miguel's eyes slide to the door lock on the car. The button had been pushed to Open, which meant the door wasn't latched. As if he were clutching the neck of a violin, Miguel's fingers wrapped around the chrome door handle.

"Yes, our Jeep will be fixed by three o'clock today. In the meantime, we've seen most of the park. It's been incredible."

Slowly, quietly, Miguel released the buckle of his seat belt with his left hand, so gently it didn't make a sound. He was going to run, Jack knew it. If the news was bad, Miguel would bolt out of the car and take off just as he had so many times before, disappearing into the undergrowth until he could find another way to Seattle. Maybe he'd hitch a ride with another family. Or maybe he'd climb into a van with bad people like Max and Terry. Then, once more, Miguel would become a shadow. Jack couldn't let him do it. But it didn't seem fair to keep him prisoner. He'd come so far....

"So you've heard from the Immigration Service?" She shot Miguel a look, and then continued, "What did they say?"

"Uh huh. Uh huh. I can understand their problem. Yes, of course."

Miguel's entire body stiffened as he leaned closer to the door. Jack tensed himself to grab him, wondering if he should....

"And the teacher in Seattle, Crecensia Álvarez, what did she say?" Olivia pressed.

Jack could see the whites all the way around Miguel's eyes as he took in a wavering breath.

"She did! Oh, Ms. Lopez, that's marvelous. Yes, of course, I'll let you tell him. He'll be so happy! Miguel, I believe this call is for you!"

When she handed the phone to Miguel, Jack saw the look on his mother's face; he raised his palm to give her, and then his sister, a high five.

"I knew they wouldn't send him back!" Ashley exclaimed. "I just knew it!"

"Well, you were the only one. It was nip and tuck with the people at Immigration, but they finally consented." Olivia reached over and gave Steven a quick hug before exclaiming, "It's all set. Miguel's mother gave permission for him to live with his teacher, and the teacher agreed. He's going to Seattle, just like he wanted. That was a brilliant idea you kids had to get Miguel's story to the *Missoulian* newspaper."

"And then the wire services picked it up," Steven added, "so the story went out all over the country."

"But," Ashley interrupted, as Miguel chattered away in Spanish over the cell phone, "how's he going to get to Seattle? We can't just stick him on a bus, not after all he's done for Jack and me."

Olivia grinned at her children. "You think we were just going to dump him? No way! Your father and I already decided that if things worked out—"

"Right," Steven finished. "We're gonna drive him there, all the way to the front door of his new home. We figured we owe him that much."

Miguel was still chatting happily in Spanish to Ms. Lopez—in his own language, that boy was quite a talker. Jack shook his head, hardly daring to believe the good news. Miguel was safe now. He would have the life he wanted, and the Landons were a part of getting him where he wanted to be.

Every single person in the car seemed to glow with a patina of happiness that a lens couldn't capture, but it was there, just the same.

A truly perfect picture.

AFTERWORD

Glacier National Park has a special place in many visitors' hearts because it is home to grizzly bears. Certainly, a hike in the park would not be the same for me if it were not grizzly country. The presence of bears sharpens my senses and makes me pay attention to small things I might otherwise overlook. Of course, I always yell "hey bear" when I'm hiking to let the bears know I'm coming so I don't surprise one. To check if a bear has passed my way recently, I like to search for tracks in muddy sections of the trail. I've developed an eye for trees that bears like to scratch their backs on. The bark is sometimes worn smooth and covered with hair from years of bear rubbing. I'm always on the look-out for bear droppings because they tell me what the bears are eating. They also help me identify the bears with DNA fingerprinting techniques!

In *The Hunted,* Ashley is afraid to be in Glacier

National Park after reading a book about two women who were killed by grizzly bears there in 1967. And who can blame her? There aren't too many things more frightening to imagine. But the bears involved in those attacks had lost their innate desire to avoid people because they had been fed human food. Over the past 30 years, we have learned a lot about how to retain the natural feeding behavior and shyness of bears by keeping our food and garbage away from them.

Unfortunately, many people believe all bears are bloodthirsty killers. Nothing could be further from the truth. As much as 90 percent of the diet of Glacier's bears consists of leaves, berries, and roots. Grizzlies spend a lot of time grazing on grass just like cows! Many of the animals they eat, such as ants and moths, are small. Bears do everything they can to steer clear of people. By using their keen ears and amazing sense of smell, they detect our presence and usually quietly slip away before we even know they're there. But you could encounter a bear at close range if it is windy or a rushing mountain stream drowns out your noise. When this happens, the bear is just as frightened as you are! In an instant, the grizzly must decide whether it is safe to run away or whether it must stay and defend itself. It almost always decides to leave.

As powerful and frightening as grizzly bears can be, their fate rests in our hands. Through habitat destruction and hunting, humans are capable of exterminating zlies. In fact, the population south of Canada almost became extinct earlier this century. Grizzlies survive here now only because we have decided to share some of our land with them. In a few national parks and wilderness areas grizzly bears continue to impart the aura of untamed nature these places were created to preserve.

As an ecologist, I have been privileged to study the fascinating lives of grizzly bears and black bears in Glacier and Yellowstone National Parks for the past 22 years. Each is etched in my memory by my connection with these remarkable animals—1977: crawling into my first bear den to try it on for size (it was unoccupied at the time!); 1979: visiting a high mountain forest in April and finding six-foot-deep holes in the snow where bears had dug down to raid squirrel caches of pine nuts; 1983: watching from a ridge as a grizzly and black bears ate huckleberries on a slope turned crimson and gold with the arrival of fall; 1990: taking a spring bike ride up Going-to-the-Sun Road and spying a grizzly bear and her two cubs sliding on a distant snowfield. I hope all of you someday will have the opportunity to experience the magic of grizzly country.

Kate Kendall
Leader, Greater Glacier Bear DNA Project
Glacier National Park

To learn more about bears in Glacier National Park, visit
http://www.mesc.usgs.gov/glacier/staff/Kendall.html

ABOUT THE AUTHORS

An award-winning mystery writer and an award-winning science writer—who are also mother and daughter—are working together on Mysteries in Our National Parks!

Alane (Lanie) Ferguson's first mystery, *Show Me the Evidence,* won the Edgar Award, given by the Mystery Writers of America.

Gloria Skurzynski's *Almost the Real Thing* won the American Institute of Physics Science Writing Award.

Lanie lives in Elizabeth, Colorado. Gloria lives in Salt Lake City, Utah. To work together on a novel, they connect by phone, fax, and e-mail and "often forget which one of us wrote a particular line."

Gloria's e-mail: gloriabooks@qwest.net
Her Web site: http://gloriabooks.com
Lanie's e-mail: aferguson@sprynet.com

DON'T MISS—

WOLF STALKER
MYSTERY #1
Fast-paced adventure has the Landons on the trail
of an injured wolf in Yellowstone National Park.

CLIFF-HANGER
MYSTERY #2
Jack's desire to help the headstrong Lucky Deal
brings him face-to-face with a hungry cougar in
Mesa Verde National Park.

DEADLY WATERS
MYSTERY #3
Jack and Ashley's efforts to save an injured manatee
involve them in a thrilling chase through the Everglades.

RAGE OF FIRE
MYSTERY #4
This simmering tale of mystery, adventure, and science
is set in Hawaii Volcanoes National Park.

COMING SOON—

GHOST HORSES
MYSTERY #6

The world's largest nonprofit scientific and educational organization, the National Geographic Society
was founded in 1888 "for the increase and diffusion of geographic knowledge." Since then it has
supported scientific exploration and spread information to its more than eight million members
worldwide. The National Geographic Society educates and inspires millions every day through
magazines, books, television programs, videos, maps and atlases, research grants, the National
Geographic Bee, teacher workshops, and innovative classroom materials. The Society is supported
through membership dues, charitable donations, and income from the sale of its educational products.
Members receive NATIONAL GEOGRAPHIC magazine—the Society's official journal—discounts on
Society products and other benefits. For more information about the National Geographic Society,
its educational programs and publications, and ways to support its work,
please call 1-800-NGS-LINE (647-5463), or write to the following address:

NATIONAL GEOGRAPHIC SOCIETY
1145 17th Street N.W.
Washington, D.C. 20036-4688
U.S.A.

Visit the Society's Web site: www.nationalgeographic.com